How to Survive
ABSOLUTELY ANYTHING

HELAINE BECKER

Fitzhenry & Whiteside

For Marsha Skrypuch, who took me to lunch one day and
told me I had to write this book. I guess I owe her a
lunch now. And maybe a big fat thank you, too. — H.B.

Text copyright © 2012 Helaine Becker

Published in Canada by Fitzhenry & Whiteside, 195 Allstate Parkway,
Markham, Ontario L3R 4T8
Published in the United States by Fitzhenry & Whiteside, 311 Washington
Street, Brighton, Massachusetts 02135

www.fitzhenry.ca   godwit@fitzhenry.ca
10 9 8 7 6 5 4 3 2 1

Library and Archives Canada Cataloguing in Publication
Becker, Helaine, 1961-
How to survive absolutely anything / Helaine Becker.
ISBN 978-1-55455-188-0
I. Title.
PS8553.E295532H69 2012   jC813'.6   C2012-902327-2

Publisher Cataloging-in-Publication Data (U.S)
Becker, Helaine.
How to survive absolutely anything / Helaine Becker.
[200] p. : cm.
ISBN: 978-1-55455-188-0 (pbk.)
1. Teenagers – Juvenile fiction. 2. Interpersonal relations -- Juvenile
fiction. 3. High schools -- Juvenile fiction. I. Title.
[Fic] dc23 PZ7.B435Ho 2012

Fitzhenry & Whiteside acknowledges with thanks the Canada Council for
the Arts, and the Ontario Arts Council for their support of our publishing
program. We acknowledge the financial support of the Government of
Canada through the Canada Book Fund (CBF) for our publishing activities.

Canada Council   Conseil des Arts
for the Arts   du Canada

ONTARIO ARTS COUNCIL
CONSEIL DES ARTS DE L'ONTARIO

Cover design by Daniel Choi
Interior design by CommTech Unlimited
Cover images courtesy of ShutterStock & Sean C. Go
Illustrations by Francesco Paonessa
Printed in Canada by Webcom

ANCIENT FOREST™
FRIENDLY

trees were saved
for our forests

Preserving our environment

Fitzhenry & Whiteside Limited chose to print the pages of this
book on recycled paper and saved these resources[1]:

energy	water	greenhouse gases	solid waste
13 million BTUs	55,446 L	1,473 kg	421 kg

Printed by Webcom Inc. on
Legacy TB Natural 100% post-consumer waste.

98 %

FSC
www.fsc.org
MIX
Paper from
responsible sources
FSC® C004071

[1]Estimates were made using the Environmental Defense Paper Calculator.

BONNIE'S BLAHBLAHBLAH JOURNAL

As in - this is private. Keep yer mitts off.
That means you too, CARTER!!

Well, we finally got the blog up and online. It only took about a thousand years longer than it should have because my mom needed to double check every single detail to make sure "we didn't do anything careless, better safe than sorry and all that, you know dear," (fake laugh, fake laugh). She's so over-protective. I may be the baby of the family, but it's like she still thinks I'm six and need my mittens on strings or I might lose them between the door and the back fence.

And then Carter decided he wanted to soup it up, add some totally <u>kewl</u> graphics, and the whole thing froze and I wanted to beat his brains in and Mom had to sit me down and remind me that Carter has not adjusted as well as I have (Triple HA!) to the new living arrangements, that he had a lot more space and privacy over at his old place and I should cut him some slack. And I'm thinking if he's used to privacy he should "get" the concept of privacy and stay out of my stuff, but he's nothing but a spoiled private school geek and oh joy of joys, my own, dear, exactly-the-same-age-as-me new brother. God, I envy my older sister, Celia. She moved out last year, leaving me and

Joe to cope with the new arrangements all on our lonesome.

Anyway, long story short, Jen and I posted our first blog post and now we just have to wait and see if we get any hits. And just maybe, _maybe_, somebody will send us in a question!

HOW TO SURVIVE ABSOLUTELY ANYTHING

with Bonnie and Jen

 o OK, so if you've clicked on this blog you probably want to know how to survive something terrible.

 • And if you are in middle school or junior high, guaranteed, something terrible has happened to you. Is happening to you right now. Or is about to happen to you.

 o How do we know?

• Because we've been there. Definitely been there.

 o Every terrible thing that can happen to a person in middle school or junior high has happened to one of us. Yes-siree-bob. We two otherwise normal teens are a walking catalogue of possible middle school disasters.

 • Getting picked on by head cases? Yup.

 o Extended periods of severe klutziness? Yes.

• Being abused by wacko teachers?

Uh-huh.

○ Dysfunctional family making it hard to concentrate on school work? Oh yeah.

• Experiencing puberty in full view of the public?

wincing Yes.

○ Bad grades? Bad moods? Bad hair? Bad karma? Check, check, check, check. I particularly enjoy how these items all frequently roll together to produce one cosmically awful day after another. Don't you?

• Not really, Bonnie.

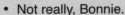
Anyway, between the two of us, we've just about covered off every rotten piece of teenage angst possible. Which is why, now that we are in grade 9 and have survived it all, we feel one hundred percent qualified—no, more like one billion percent qualified, to give advice on how to survive absolutely anything and everything.

Anything.

○ Yup. Anything.

Yours Truly, Bonnie & Jen

My Profile

Name: Bonnie B.

Location: Somewhere in Canada. It's a major city with a tall tower in it.

Age/Sex: 14/F

My Interests

Hobbies:

Healthy Living (Fitness, Food, the Environment), Writing my own comic strip. Studying pores close up in mirror to discover if a new zit is about to erupt to ruin my life.

Favourite Movies:

Hugo, Toy Story 3, Fifty First Dates.

Favourite Music:

Mumford & Sons, Green Day, Chili Peppers, Molly Johnson (awesome jazz—check it out)

Favourite Celebrities:

I don't gawk over celebrities. Why should I? They don't gawk over me.

Bonnie.B

Favourite Food:
I know I SHOULD say soy but I adore chocolate and pizza.

Favourite Animal:
The Puffin. They are way cuter than penguins and 100% Canadian.

Famous Lines:
"What's so funny about peace, love, and understanding?" "Sometimes, I just hate my ovaries", "Why do boys have to be so cute AND so dumb at the same time?"

Favourite Colour:
Happy—Face Yellow

Turn-ons:
If he can make me laugh, he's 99% there.

Turn-offs:
When he's brain dead; sports freaks; acne on back; Neanderthal ideas on what girls' roles should be.

Buddies:
Jen, of course.

Future Career:
Fitness Trainer; Marine Biologist; Greenpeace Activist.

My Profile

Name: Jennifer W.

Location: Somewhere in Canada.
We're hockey fanatics
here. Sorry—that's not
much of a hint is it?

Age/Sex: 14/F

My Interests

Hobbies:
Cycling, Volleyball, Hockey (I'm a major Leafs fan.)

Favourite Movies:
Slumdog Millionaire, Pirates of the Caribbean, Oceans 11,
Oceans 12, Oceans 13, Oceans Anything—I love bank heist
movies, heh heh.

Favourite Music:
Chili Peppers, Mumford & Sons, Molly Johnson (If I didn't
put Molly here Bonnie would kill me)

Favourite Celebrities:
Johnny Depp and Brad Pitt when they don't talk. Hugh
Jackman when he doesn't sing.

Jen.Jen

Favourite Food:
Nachos. Warm brownies w ice cream and fudge sauce.

Favourite Animal:
Golden Retriever Puppies.

Famous Lines:
"Good times...good times." "Oops!—Sorry!" (I'm kind of a klutz.)

Favourite Colour:
Hot pink and lime green—together

Turn-ons:
Nice hair, nice eyes, nice smile, being a nice person.

Turn-offs:
Self-centred jerks can stay away. FAR away. And anyone wearing Axe. Yuck.

Buddies:
Bonnie, of course.

Future Career:
Anything that does not involve health care or child care. Maybe a bush pilot.

o We're both grade 9 students at Our Lady of Torture High School. You probably know it. Heck, you're probably our classmate.

 • You'd probably even be our best friend if Bonnie and I weren't each other's best friends already. We've been best friends since Bonnie barfed on me in preschool.

 o It wasn't barf. It was a very little spit up.

 • Whatever, Bon. It was gross. But I got over it. Sort of. Twitch twitch. :)

 o We *do not* look like twins. I don't care what all those idiots out there say. We both have light brown hair that is naturally dead straight, but Jen's is closer to Clairol's Light Brown 116 and mine is more like Light Golden Brown 116A. And I don't have bangs and Jen does.

 • And Bonnie's eyes are green-brown and mine are brown-green. Plus, if we were cartoon characters, her eyes would be shaped like big round 0's and mine would be sideways-y arrows.

 o Since we do not have black outlines or hair that stands up in spiky anti-gravity 'dos, another way to tell us apart is that Jen's boobs are bigger, especially when she's about to get her period.

 • And Bonnie's mouth is bigger, especially like when she's alive.

 ○ I have about seventy-six brothers and sisters. You guessed it—blended family. Half-sibs, step-sibs, half-step-step sibs, half-sibs of your half-sibs who are not your sibs at all but somehow wind up barfing on your bed anyway.

 • It's always about the barf with you, Bonnie. :)
I have only one sister and she is two and a half. (Come to think of it, it's always about barf with Julia too.) :D
Unlike Bonnie with her giant family (FEE FI FO FUM), my family is small—only Julia and my mom. My mom won't let me call her "Mom"—she prefers it if I call her Tina. Which is only odd if you know that my mom's name is Colette and she has never even met anyone named Tina.
But hey, if she wants to be called Tina, why not? Maybe I'd rather be a Tina than a Colette, too, if I were her. Her life pretty well stinks.
For the record, I live in total chaos.

 ○ And I live in total chaos, too. But somehow…

We have both managed to survive. *Fabulously*, if we do say so ourselves.

Jen, you are fabulous.

 • Bonnie, you are fabulous.

There. We said it ourselves.

And because we have survived with such incredible *fabulosity*, that is why we can give *you* such good advice on how to survive whatever crappola *you* are going through.

So send us your questions. We will answer them. Quickly. Effectively. And without—we promise— even a *hint* of barf.

Click <u><HERE></u> to contact Bonnie and Jen with your questions on how to survive absolutely anything.

I should really be paying attention to Mrs. Weiner right now, but honestly, who cares how many electrons can fit into each atomic orbit? I bet Mrs. Weiner doesn't even care. Besides, I'm spinny enough on my own, ha ha. Who needs atomic particles whizzing around in your brain when you've got your own personal Tilt-a-whirl head? {STORY. OF. MY. LIFE.}

Besides, I can't stop thinking about the blog, and also about that stupid starfish story mom tells me whenever she's wearing her " we all have to make an effort, because each and every one of us matters" social, consciousness hat. It keeps rolling and rolling around in my head like a hundred spinning electrons.

So here's how it goes:

Millions of starfish wash up on a beach. There's this boy and he's walking along the shore. Picking up the starfish, one by one. Then he throws them, one by one, back into the ocean.

A man puts his hand on the boy's shoulder. No, not a creepo, just a guy.

"Son," the man said, "there are so many starfish on the beach. What you're doing won't make any difference."

15

The kid looks the guy in the eye." Sure it will—to that starfish," he says.

Ok, it's a cute story. But there's more to it than that. If you stop and think about it for a sec, it can give you shivers. It's sorta—deep. <OCEAN JOKE Ba-dum pum>

So here's why I can't get this woo-woo story out of my mind:

What I'm thinking is—and maybe it's kind of arrogant to think this?—but maybe Jen and I are like that starfish boy. And our blog? It's like the starfish beach. And maybe, just maybe, we can make a difference to one stranded starfish out there...?

I know Carter would roll his eyes at me (naah—too much work) and Joe would probably thunk me in the head with a pillow and Mom would probably make some glorious speech that completely missed the point. But I feel really, really good about this blog. Is that totally stupid or what?

I can't WAIT to check the blog to see if we have any q's but I promised Jen I wouldn't look without her and I won't break my promise even though IT...IS...KILLING...ME!!!!

SURVIVAL SKILL #1:

PROPERLY EQUIP YOURSELF FOR THE SITUATION.

Jen was already at their lockers when Bonnie got there the next morning.

"Did you check it?" Jen blurted out before Bonnie could even say "Hi."

"Hey! Relax! Lemme get my coat off at least!" Bonnie replied with a grin. "And for your information, the answer is no. I promised I wouldn't, didn't I? Though I did tweet and post news to teen sites, and Facebook it like mad. No point in having a blog if no one knows about it, right?"

"Truth. C'mon then! Let's get this junk put away and go see if your spreading-the-word skills worked."

They stuffed their books into their lockers and practically ran to the Media Centre. Jen flicked on their favourite computer—the one farthest from the door. The one someone had hacked so kids could get around the 'prohibited actions' filters.

"Funny how in this blabbermouth-ridden school, no one has ratted out this computer to a teacher yet," Jen whispered.

"Amazing but true," Bonnie concurred. "Even morons can keep a secret when it matters."

"Hurry up, hurry up, you stupid hourglass," Jen muttered at the screen, drumming her fingers on the tabletop while the PC took its sweet time booting up.

Bonnie eyed her friend critically. Jen's hair needed a wash and she had dark circles under her eyes. Plus she was wearing her ugliest outfit—a baggy sweatshirt in lime green with matching track pants. It made her look like a newt. One speckled with lint.

"No offense, but you look awful," Bonnie said.

Jen grimaced. "Gee, thanks." She sank back in her chair, pulled the elastic off her ponytail, and tried to smooth her hair. "I fell asleep when I was getting Julia ready for bed last night. So I never got to do any homework or anything. When I woke up this morning, I totally freaked. I bagged the shower and raced through my math while I ate my toast."

"Ick. What happened to Tina?"

"Remind me never to become a nurse. Those sick people are just so insensitive, *ar ar.* She had to do overtime again. I don't even know what time she got in. Oh—look. We're up and running, girlfriend. Type in the address!"

Bonnie swivelled her chair around and keyed in the blog URL. A few seconds later, the familiar purple-and-grey screen began to load.

"Omigod! There's a question!" Jen squeaked, bouncing up and down in her seat. "Turn the screen! I can't see it!"

Bonnie nudged the monitor around so Jen could get a better view. They read together:

Dear Bonnie and Jen,

  I checked out your blog and thought you sounded really cool. I hope you can help me. I really like this guy, but I don't know if he likes me. We flirt constantly and always joke around, pretending we're going out and stuff. Our friends tell us we'd make a perfect couple, and he just laughs and says, "Yeah." I don't know what it means, if he likes me or if he doesn't. What should I do?

—In-Limbo Queen

"Hot tamale," breathed Jen. "An honest-to-dog problem question."

"What do we tell her to do?" Bonnie wondered out loud, her mind already churning furiously.

"Do you think it's for real?" Jen asked.

"I dunno," Bonnie said. "But what's the diff? If it's real or not, we still have to answer it. That's what we said we'd do."

"I know," replied Jen, "but that was when it was still all kind of imaginary."

"So let's pretend it still *is* imaginary," Bonnie answered confidently. She set her fingers firmly on the keyboard. "What do we want to say?"

"Why don't we leave it 'til lunch break? Then we can both log on and do it the way we did the first post, back and forth, both at the same time. Besides, I want to think about what I want to say for a bit."

"OK. But Jen! Isn't it the *greatest*? I mean, our

19

very first hit on our very first blog! Woo-HOO!" Bonnie raised her palms for a double high-five.

Jennifer smiled wide. She reached up and laced her fingers through Bonnie's, giving both hands a *rah-rah* shake.

"Yeah, it's as good as it gets. At 8:47 in the morning, anyway. Now I got to get going. Mr. Oki's going to tear a strip off me if I don't finish my homework before class starts in exactly thirteen, no, twelve minutes."

SURVIVAL SKILL #2:

ADDRESS THE PROBLEM FROM VARIOUS ANGLES.

"Well? What do you think?" Jen asked, her head tipped to one side as she studied the screen.

"Do you mean, 'Do I think we sound like morons and totally full of it?' or 'Does what we wrote sound half-way decent and maybe like we actually know what we're talking about?'" Bonnie said.

"Um, yeah, that's about the size of it," Jen said. She was chewing with deep concentration on a hangnail and swivelling back and forth in her chair. "Both. What do you think?"

Bonnie re-read their first post for about the fifth time.

 ° Dear Limbo Queen,

He so totally likes you.

 • Whoa, Nellie! And Bonnie, don't say that your name is not Nellie. The expression means, "Slow Down, Girl!" and that's what you've got to do.

21

You have to understand, Limbo Queen, that Bonnie is a complete and utter romantic fool. And an optimist. She sees the world through rose-coloured contact lenses.

 o OK, so I am a little bit rainbows and butterflies and unicorns. But I'm also extremely logical. Call me Data, all you Star Trek geeks. So let's look at this rationally. Why would anyone—ANYONE—pretend to like you as more than just a friend if they didn't? Wouldn't that just be stupid?
So unless he is a complete and utter moron—and OK, he is a guy, so that is always a very real possibility—the only logical answer is: he likes you. And he's just shy or afraid that you'll reject him, so he's playing it safe by playing the game.

 • Not so fast, my pink-eyed, robotic pal. There is one other possibility: Like, maybe he's gay?

 o Wow—I never even thought of that. Your mind definitely works in interesting ways!

 • Maybe so, but that's what you love about me, isn't it? *eye bat, eye bat*
Besides, Limbo Queen should consider *all* the options. And my suggestion isn't really so far fetched. Remember Mark? The guy that was friends

with your brother Joe? How you thought he was so cute and all?

 ○ Yeah...

 • And then he came out and you were all crushed because he had been so extra nice to you and acted like he liked you.

 ○ I *was* only 12, Jen.

 • Whatever. My point is that maybe Limbo Queen's Mr. "Maybe I Do Maybe I Don't" is doing the same thing. Maybe he's gay and he likes her—just not in "that way"—but because he's gay, it doesn't really occur to him that she might be misinterpreting his intentions. So he's kinda sending the wrong signals.

 ○ OK. I see what you're saying. Gay is a possibility. But I still think it's a stretch. For my two cents, I believe he really likes her and is a weenie. Not *that* many guys are gay, after all. But *lots* of them are weenies.

 • Fair enough. Now that we've laid out the possibilities, I guess Limbo Queen's first step will be to decide for herself.

o So what advice should we give her on what to DO, then?????

 • She should ask him.

 o You mean like, "Excuse me, doll face, but I can't tell: are you hot for me or queer?"

 • Maybe that's not the all time best approach, *chica*. If he *does* like her, I'm thinkin' that he doesn't want to put himself out there because he's scared of getting burned. Maybe Limbo Queen can get the ball rolling by suggesting that she isn't kidding entirely when she flirts with him. Once that door has been opened, maybe he'll nudge it further open with his toe…

 o His toe? Isn't that kinda kinky?

 • Now who's being 'interesting'?

 o OK, so let's say Limbo Queen gets Lover Boy alone, they're hangin' out, just chillin'. He says something flirty. She says, "You know, I'm not entirely kidding when I say I like you in a more-than-a-friend way…" and he freaks out and backs off. What does she do now?

• That would totally suck, wouldn't it? But all is not lost! Not with Jen and Bonnie to help you through it! This is what you do. Leave a very long awkward pause. This will allow your stomach to stop heaving. Then start laughing. Try to make it sound real if you can, fake/forced laughter is just so awful. If you can't do the real-sounding laugh, skip it. Just bonk him over the head with a pillow or something and say, "Kidding! Omigod—did you believe me? You are *such* a geek."

Then continue on as if nothing happened.

 ○ That could work. And of course there is the other possibility….

 • *Ding DING!*

 ○ He doesn't freak but instead looks you deep in the eyes and says, "You know, *I'm* not totally kidding either…."

 • Well, now you're talking.

 ○ Listen up, Limbo Queen: I've got a heap of brothers so I can tell you that most guys need YOU to tell THEM what to do most of the time. Hey, your fly is open—zip it. Hey, you smell—take a shower. Hey, leave a donut for someone else, Hoover.

So expect that if this marvy moment actually comes your way, you'll have to tell this guy what to do, too. You're gonna have to point out to him, "Hey! Stupid! We just admitted after like fifty-six years that we *like* each other! THIS is the part where you kiss the girl!" Otherwise you might just wind up looking at each other all goofy-like and never...you know.

 • Get boyfriendy and girlfriendy.

 o Yeah. So make it official. You will figure out a way to make it happen. If worse comes to worst, grab him by the ears and plant one on him.
And don't worry if you mash noses the first time. Everyone does.

 • Good luck, Limbo Queen. I sincerely hope for your sake he's not gay or psycho or as stupid as rotting wood chips.

 o Me 2. And please, please, pretty please let us know what happens. And remember, whatever does happen…

YOU WILL SURVIVE!!!!!!
XXXs and OOOs
Jen and Bonnie

Bonnie swung her legs up under her so she was kneeling in her chair. Then she reached out and grabbed Jen's seat to halt her restless swivelling dead.

Bringing her face close to Jen's, Bonnie forced Jen's eyes to meet her own. "Honestly? I think it's freaking awesome," she said.

"Then do it," Jennifer said, biting her lower lip.

"You got it."

Bonnie whipped around, back to the PC.

"Are you sure?" she asked, hand poised on the mouse.

"I guess so," Jen said, assiduously peeling back a corner of the desk's laminated edge. One lank lock of hair obscured her face.

Bonnie slid the cursor over to "Post."

"Last chance…."

Jen nodded. Bonnie pressed Enter.

Limbo Queen's advice whooshed its way out to never-ending cyberspace.

So there I am, just sitting in my room, minding my own thing, doing my homework and stuff, when who comes bouncing in but Carter.

HATE HATE HATE
DORK HATE
CAR-TURD

"Nice of you to knock," I say, dripping sarcasm, but Carter doesn't get it. Or more to the point, doesn't care even if he does get it, because in I'm so-good-looking-everybody-loves-me Carter's world, "What's mine is mine, what's yours is mine."

"Hey," he says, which in Carter-speak, passes for a witty comment.

"Bye," I say.

"Watcha doin'?" he says.

I give him the "Are you a total idiot?" face—after all, my homework is all spread out around me—but he is unfazed. I begin to wonder what kind of amazing boy-in-a-bubble childhood he must have had to be so oblivious to the world around him.

Joe, Celia, and I always got an earful of "Do you think the world revolves around you?" and "Treat everyone with courtesy and respect!" when we were kids. We didn't actually ever pay attention to M & D then, but you know, after fourteen years, some of it leaks into your brain.

Apparently, Carter has never heard this kind of advice once. Which is kind of weird because Otto, his dad, is actually a pretty decent guy. Carter's mother, on the other hand, is clearly an escapee from a mental institution (another story). But Otto must have told Carter at some point in his life to smarten up. You would think.

Apparently not. The upshot is that Carter is, like, the most selfish person on the face of the earth. And his part of the earth is, unfortunately, smack dab next to mine.

So I go back to my geography work, ignoring the fact that Car-turd has now plunked himself down on the end of my bed and has almost sat on my feet, which I have had to squinch up under me to get them away from him. He doesn't budge. In fact, he leans back against the wall, stretching out and putting his hands behind his head so his ugly hairy pits are, like, front and centre in my face. Did I mention he isn't wearing a shirt? Ick.

"Do you mind?" I say in my most frostiest ice-queen tone.

"Whuh?" he says.

I go, "You're ruding me out, Car."

He raises his eyebrows. Looks left and right at himself and starts to chuckle.

"Sorry," he says. "Didn't mean to offend." He puts his hands in his lap. Thank heavens for small favours.

Then he asks me "how everything was shakin'," how the blog was going, what I'm up to etc.

I just stare at him.

Then he asks, "Been to any cool parties or anything, or do the nuns not let you out?" and he juts out his perfect superhero chin, and lets his Movie Star Blue eyes twinkle in that, "aren't I charming, even when I'm being a tool?" way that makes other people bow and genuflect whenever he walks by.

When will he learn his golden boy act will never ever, ever, EVER work on me?

ANSWER: NEVER EVER EVER PYOOOOOK!

"Are you done yet, Carter?" I say, sighing, "I really have to finish this homework."

But Carter still won't get the hint. He just keeps looking at me with those "please like me" eyes and flapping his yap.

"Actually, Bonbon," (Yes, he called me

30

Bonbon. Ugh.)" I was wondering if you and maybe a couple of your friends would want to come to a dance up on the Hill on Friday."

I blinked a couple of times. Felt my stomach lurch.

"Carter, did you just invite me to one of your oh-so-exclusive Prep School par-tays? What's the matter? All the private school girls have chlamydia or something?"

Carter threw his hands up in the air. Ugh—those pits again.

Then he started on this rant about how our combo parents wanted us to "get along" and he was just trying to be nice. You know, like, "making an effort." And if I was going to be all snarkerella he wouldn't bother wasting his time next time.

Then he lurched to his feet, shaking the bed so hard my teeth rattled, and stomped in a gorilla huff to the door. The weird thing, though was, once he got there, he didn't keep going. He just slumped against the door frame, and gave me this disappointed look. I swear he even looked hurt, which I admit really freaked me out. I mean, since when did Carter the Cosmetically Enhanced Apeboy have actual human feelings? I didn't think his baboon-brain was capable of them.

I felt a big nasty lump form in my throat.

Then he says, "Would it kill you, Bon, to say, 'Sure, Carter, that would be great! It would be fun to go to a party with you?'" And he turns to leave, still shaking his head.

I am not proud to say I relented. I took a deep breath and told him he was right (I KNOW!) and then I even offered to see if Jen would want to come. She'll kill me but NO WAY I'm going through with this by myself.

Carter smiled his patented movie-star perfect, Crest-white, orthodontics-expensive smile.

"Awesome, Bons!" he says. "And hey—it'll be fun."

Ever the well-brought up good girl that I am, I replied, "Thanks for asking, Carter."

How does he do that all the time? Makes ME feel like I'm the one who's a total twit???

b.o.n.n.i.e :)   10:20PM

U wil never Bleve what just happnd. Carter invited us to a parT at Prep H.

JEN.⁺ <3   10:21PM

RU kidding!

b.o.n.n.i.e :) 10:21PM

X my Heart & hope 2 Di

JEN.⁺ <3   10:21PM

He's joking?

b.o.n.n.i.e :)   10:22PM

I don't think so. He askd me 2 bring friends. I sed Id ask u.

JEN.⁺ <3   10:22PM

When?

b.o.n.n.i.e :)   10:23PM

Friday. Is Tina working?

JEN.⁺ <3   10:24PM

Let me check.

JEN.* <3   10:29PM
No. She has the nite off. So I
cn go with u if u want me 2

b.o.n.n.i.e :)   10:29PM
Do u think we should go?

JEN.* <3   10:29PM
Y not?

b.o.n.n.i.e :)   10:30PM
U no Carter. And u no his
friends...

JEN.* <3   10:30PM
Ur mom will be ticked at u if
you say no.

b.o.n.n.i.e :)   10:30PM
Ur so rite.

JEN.* <3   10:31PM
& Carters not rly so bad.
Bsides ther r other BOYS @
Stupid Rich Boys Get High than
jus Carter & the Cretins. Sum
mite even be ok.

b.o.n.n.i.e :)   10:32PM
XLNt point.

JEN.* <3   10:32PM
So we go?

b.o.n.n.i.e :)   10:33PM
Im on the fence.

JEN.* <3   10:33PM
I say we go.

b.o.n.n.i.e :)   10:34PM
If u think its ok then OK.

JEN.* <3   10:34PM
In that Kse: *Fashn emergNC!*

b.o.n.n.i.e :)   10:34PM
Ill call Celia

JEN.* <3   10:35PM
UR brilliant. L8R BF

b.o.n.n.i.e :)   10:35PM
Luvya

SURVIVAL SKILL #3:

DEFINITELY DRESS FOR SUCCESS.

"**O**migod, we have to get you girls drop-dead gorgeous," Celia gushed when Bonnie called her with the news of the party. "Which won't be hard, especially if all those other girls are going to be those private school sticks. They might have buckets of cash, but they have zero fashion sense. They're sheeple, not people. I mean, Burberry? Come on."

Celia agreed to pick the girls up after school and drive them downtown to Kensington Market, where Courage My Love was sandwiched between a fish store and a Salvadorean espresso bar. According to Celia, 'Courage' was the last word in vintage clothing stores. It was Cool Cubed.

At 3:02 PM, Bonnie and Jen were sprawled out on the sparse grass in front of their school, waiting impatiently for Celia to arrive.

Bonnie clapped her palms together in tiny little happyclaps. "We're going to have such a good time!" she squealed. "I haven't seen Celia in, jeesh, I don't know how long. Too long."

"I guess she doesn't get much chance to come into

town anymore," Jen said, idly running her fingers through the yellowing crabgrass. She yanked out a piece and started peeling it into two narrow strands.

"No—she says she has a really heavy class schedule this year. Plus a thesis to write. University isn't all party party, it seems," Bonnie said with a rueful nod.

"You're still lucky," Jen sighed. "Having such a cool big sis and all. You know I always wanted one: Someone to hang out with, play "beauty pageant" with, teach me how to make my Sims houses as cool as the other kids' Sims houses..."

"Someone to show you how to fix your hair so you didn't look like a dork..." Bonnie punched her lightly on the arm.

"You know what I mean," Jen said.

"Yeah. I do. But believe me, being a little sis wasn't always so great. You know I looked up to her soooo much—she was like this big glamorpuss princess, who got to stay up late and go out on dates with guys who *shaved*. And I was just this little *twerp*, with pigtails and a lisp. She didn't always have time for me."

"Five years is a pretty big age difference. I mean, when she was our age, you were, like, nine. That's practically a different planet."

"Tell me about it," Bonnie said with a roll of her eyes. "Like you and Julia. Hey! How about that, Jen? *You* get to be the cool big sis she looks up to!"

"Rah," Jennifer said. She tossed her torn strips of crabgrass into the air as if they were confetti. "But you also had Joe. I've always been sort of jealous of that, too."

Bonnie reached over and brushed a straw-coloured piece of grass off Jennifer's cheek.

"Well, don't be. I mean, not that there's anything wrong with Joe, as far as brothers go. But it would have been nice to not always be like part of a matched set, like Ruby and Max. I would have wanted, just once, to have a birthday party to myself instead of having to have a doubleheader with him."

"Well, your birthdays *are* only a week apart. It only makes sense that your folks didn't want to do two parties back to back."

Bonnie snorted. "Sure. It was more practical and convenient. For them. That's why we did our swimming lessons together. Made our trips to the dentist together. Haircuts. Everything. You'd never know he was a whole year older. Or that he was a boy and I was a girl. It's like it never occurred to them that we might have different personalities or interests."

"Oh, come on, Bonnie. It wasn't that bad. You were just pissed off because you wanted to be hanging with Celia."

"OK, so you're right," Bonnie said with a grin. "Do you blame me?" She pointed to the traffic circle, where Celia's bright red Mini had just swung into sight.

"Not a bit," Jennifer said. "And whoa! That is such a freaking cool car!"

"I know. It's so...*Celia*."

Celia zipped around the circle, tooting the horn as if

to say, "SMILE, WORLD!" She spotted the girls and waved, bringing the car to a neat stop in front of them.

"Hey! My favourite duo! The Bonnie and Jennie Comedy Show!" she shouted, blowing air kisses at them through the window.

As they climbed in, Celia eyed the front of the school with open disdain.

"It doesn't look like 'Our Lady of Interminable Tedium' has changed much since I've been gone." She shifted into first gear and the little car leapt into motion. "It still looks like a prison." She made an exaggerated shudder. "Does Miss Worley still have a Taser up her ass?"

"Ohhhh...So *that* explains her eye twitch..." Jennifer said, giggling.

"If you only knew the whole story," Celia said with mock gravity. "The Taser was actually the cure."

This time, all three of them laughed.

The whole way downtown, Celia and Bonnie never quit jabbering for a second. Fortunately, Jen had been around Celia and Bonnie long enough to keep up with them. Not too many people would have ever been able to follow their cryptic conversation. It included convoluted updates on family members, environmental issues, and trends in alt music.

Finally, the discussion came around to the big party.

"So, lil' sis, and honorary lil' sis," Celia said, giving a wink and a nod to Jen via the rearview mirror, "I've been to a ton of those shindigs. This is the drill: The music is

39

always way too loud. The boys always stand on one side of the room and bray like donkeys."

"I'm familiar with the braying. I live with Carter," Bonnie said, nodding sagely.

Celia glanced sharply at Bonnie, then did a rapid shoulder check and changed lanes. "Naaah—the guys I'm thinking of make Carter look like a regular Prince Charming. Just for fun, count how many of 'em can even manage to keep the bottoms of their shirts in their pants. It's like a law: 'Thou shalt keep thy shirt untucked.'"

"Maybe it's to hide their...ahem...*groin issues*," Bonnie suggested. "I'm pretty sure that's what Joe does."

Jen's jaw dropped. Her eyes went huge and round as she collapsed in peals of hysterical laughter.

"Definitely too much information!" she shrieked.

Celia just grinned.

"Yeah. Anyhow, Bonnie's probably right. The boys probably do have groin issues. But the girls have their own issues. Like why they cackle like demented hens."

"Maybe they have *grain* issues," Bonnie said. "Like, they're afraid they'll run out of chickenfeed."

"Good one!" Celia said, giving Bonnie a high-five.

Bonnie's face went all glowy. Her specialty had always been the shotgun pun, but no one, not even Jen, ever appreciated her wit quite the way Celia did.

Celia returned to her party description. "Eventually, the boys all go over to the girls in packs. They ask the girls to dance. There will be more cackling and more braying, then some dancing.

"Most of the dancing couples won't talk to each other very much; they won't even look at each other. This is despite the fact that they will be very busy sticking their tongues down each other's throats before the night is over."

"Gross," Bonnie said.

Celia chuckled. "Well, that all depends on who the guy is, right?"

"I'm pretty sure I'd actually prefer it to be someone I actually liked," Jennifer said.

"Don't be so sure," Celia said. "There is that category of guy known as 'pretty to look at until he opens his mouth.'"

"Carter again," Bonnie said.

"Yeah, like Carter," Jen said absently, looking out the window.

"Enough about Carter," Celia said. "Now at this party, at the end of the night, you can expect most everybody—the grade 11s and 12s, anyway—will be hammered. A lot of clothing will go missing. A lot of puke will get deposited in expensive landscaping and a couple of pricey cars will get dented."

Celia's descriptions made Bonnie feel even queasier. She just *knew* she'd be out of her depth in a scene like that. She'd never exactly been Miss Wild Party Girl.

"Gee, maybe we should stay home and watch mould grow on the bathroom tiles," she said with a quaver in her voice.

"Yeah—you don't make it sound all that fun," Jen said.

"*Au contraire.* You CAN have fun," Celia said,

41

laughing, as she angled the car into what was almost definitely an illegal parking spot. "You just have to remember that even among private school guys there are some oddballs who think most of the other kids there are idiots."

"Our kindred spirits," Jen said.

"I wouldn't go quite that far," Celia said, "but boys with partially formed brains. They'll be all right to spend the evening with. I'm sure Carter will be able to steer you in the right direction. OK, girls—the eagle has landed. Let's get shopping!"

Kensington Market had lots of neat vintage clothing shops and off-price designer shops. Soon, Celia the Vintage Clothing Queen began sharing her shopping wisdom with her newbies.

"First of all," she said, wagging her finger at them, "a lot of girls make the mistake of thinking that showing a lot of skin is sexy. Wrong. That's *slutty*. Instead, go for classic lines. And absolutely nothing uncomfortable or anything that creeps up your butt."

They scoured the racks and spent the afternoon trying on a dozen different combinations. In the end, Bonnie chose a sleeveless red dress cut low in the back but straight across the neck in front.

"I think this pin will look cool on it," Bonnie said, showing off a 'gold' brooch shaped like a cat, with 'ruby' eyes. "I found it in that case up there."

Celia and Jen gave her two thumbs up and two "double fabs".

Jen chose a vintage Pucci-style print dress with hot pink and lime green and yellow and orange—all of her favourite colours splashed together in a wild paisley pattern.

"Very shagadelic," Celia said approvingly. "All you have to do is wear large earrings and put your hair in a high ponytail and you'll look great!"

"You already look great, just like that," Bonnie assured her.

"You, too," Jen said, giving Bonnie's braid a tug, ignoring the fact that it was a total wreck from an afternoon of pulling clothes on and off over her head.

"You are a liar," Bonnie said, grinning like an idiot as she passed her Interac card to the cashier. "But I love you anyway. In fact, it's *why* I love you. I've got a thing for liars, *ha ha*."

Jennifer blew a kiss and dipped to her knee in a curtsey. "Happy to oblige," she said. "And by the way, you smell fresh as a daisy, too."

"And you both are the Queens of Cool," Celia said. "Now let's get out of here. I'm *dying* for an empanada."

SURVIVAL SKILL #4:

VICTORY—AND THE SPOILS—GO TO THE BOLD.

Bonnie and Jen dumped their shopping bags on the bed and woke up Bonnie's PC to check their blog's status. There was a post on the blog from Limbo Queen.

 Dear Bonnie and Jen,

I decided to take your advice and give it a whirl.

So we were putting away our instruments after band practice and everyone else was gone so I said, "Um, you know how we always are kidding around about how we like each other and all?"

He kinda just froze and then gulped and said, "Yeah?"

I got scared and kept putting my trumpet into my case over and over again like it wouldn't fit. And I squeaked, "I'm not entirely kidding, you know." My mouth went totally dry.

Dead silence.

Then he whispered, "Me neither."

I looked at him.

He looked at me. We both kind of caught each other's eyes and then looked away. I felt myself start to blush all the way to the roots of my hair.

"I guess that's good then, huh?" I said.

He smiled. "Yeah. Really good."

He came over to me and said, "Let me help you with that. It looks like you're having a little trouble getting that horn into its case."

Then he took my trumpet and tossed it onto the chair, dropped the case on the floor, and put his arms around me, and kissed me, right there in the middle of the band room!

"God! You have no idea how long I've wanted to do that!" he said.

So now we're "going out" and I owe it to you two! So a million thanks!!!!!!!!

 - No Longer In Limbo Queen

"Yee ha!" Bonnie shouted.

"Ding ding ding ding ding!" Jen shouted back.

"We are, like, *so good!*" Bonnie said.

Carter stuck his head in the door. "What's all the *squee*-ing about?"

Bonnie felt the blood rush to her head. "Were you listening at my door?"

Carter grinned. "I just wanted to see if you lovely ladies were talkin' about me."

Bonnie rolled her eyes. "As if."

Carter ignored her and turned his gaze to Jennifer.

"Jennifer! You're lookin' HOT!" he said, giving her the once-over.

Jen opened her mouth to reply, but before she could, Bonnie stepped in, saying, "Oh shut up, Carter. You're NOT. As usual."

Jen dropped her eyes. Her cheeks coloured.

Carter's face fell.

"Go. Now," Bonnie said in a tone that meant business.

"OK! OK!" He raised his hands in mock surrender. "Sor-RY. Just trying to be friendly."

He turned back to Jen, and his voice softened. "See you Friday, Jenjen. I'm looking forward to it." His eyes flicked to Bonnie. "Later, Bons." He waited a beat, and when she didn't answer, he turned on his heel and left.

Jen gave a noisy sigh of relief. "Whoa. That was... intense," she said once he was out of earshot.

"The Carter effect. Happens all the time around here. You'd think I'd be used to it by now, but I never do enjoy the sensation of being slimed," Bonnie said, shuddering.

"I dunno," Jen said. "Maybe he's not so bad. A doof, yes, but—"

The front door slammed. A series of distinctive bangs and thuds in the front hall that meant Joe was home. He always took the stairs three steps at a time so that the whole house shook with each footfall.

Jen seemed to forget completely about what she'd been saying. She sat up straighter, tugging at her blouse

46

and smoothing her hair as she called out a breezy, "Hiya, stranger!"

Jen had had a crush on Joe since, well, kindergarten.

Joe appeared at the bedroom door.

"Hiya back." He flipped a ball again and again into the worn pocket of his baseball glove.

"Ya mind?" he pointed to the bed. When Bonnie shook her head, he sat down and kicked back. "Were you having a 'thang' with my pal Carter? I saw him slinking back to his hole so I can only assume…"

"You got that right," Jen said with a laugh, sliding a loose strand of hair behind her ear.

"Oh, just forget about him," Joe said. "Was he giving you the gears?"

"Doesn't he always?" Bonnie said. "We just got dropped into the Carter sleazetank."

"He just came in to say hi," Jennifer said.

"Yeah, and look you over like you were a prime piece of beef round," Bonnie shot back.

"*Forget* about him," Joe said. "He's not worth it. Besides, it's celebration time. I pitched a no-hitter today!"

"Ooh, *baby*!" Bonnie said, giving him a fist bump. He was the star pitcher on his school's baseball team, and had, as they said, "high hopes."

"And—I met a special someone today…" Joe waggled his eyebrows.

Jen wrapped her arms across her chest and gave a tight smile. "Very nice."

"Aw, Jen, don't get all pouty with me. Don't I always

think of my two favourite girls? Seems Mireille—that's her—has not one, but two—*two*—brothers. We can triple date if you want. On Friday. Can you both come?"

Bonnie traded glances with Jen.

Then she groaned.

Jen groaned back.

Friday. The day they had already promised to go to the Prep H Party with Carter the Crinoid.

Reasons NOT to Go to the Dance

Carter is a major creep.

We'd definitely have more fun with Joe.

I'd like to check out the two brothers.

Carter's friends are probably creeps.

Reasons TO GO to the Dance

Mom would kill me if she knew I backed out of a promise to Carter.

I'll get to wear my great new dress.

If Joe and Mireille get along there'll be another chance to meet the brothers.

There might be people at the dance that are not, Carter's friends and therefore, are not creeps.

Jen will be there and if things get gross, we can always leave. It might be good for stories afterward.

I don't want to have to tell Carter I can't go. I don't like to think about how he'd react. It would definitely not be pretty though.

I promised. And breaking my promise would make me just as slimy as Carter.

WHICH WAY TO GO?

WHAT TO DO?

HEAD FULL OF CONFUSION —AND STRAW

49

SURVIVAL SKILL #5:

APPLY STRATEGIC THINKING TO AVOID UNNECESSARY BATTLES.

That Friday, Jen showed up at school carrying a huge striped duffle bag.

"What have you got there?" Bonnie asked, helping Jen to jam it into her locker.

"It's my dress, shoes, makeup—everything for tonight. Julia was sick all last night. Tina is, like, a total freak today. She keeps yelling at me like it's my fault the baby has a fever and won't stop crying. I don't think I can stand to go back to that today. I won't get any chance to chill or get dressed—Tina will just put me to work cleaning up dirty dishes or doing pukey baby laundry or feeding Julia.

"If I don't show after school, though, she won't be able to boss me around. She'll have to do that stuff herself for a change, without Cinderella there to pick on. So thanks for offering, girlfriend. I'm going home with you."

"Sure, of course. You know you're welcome any time," Bonnie said.

Jen slammed the door to her locker shut with a decisive clang. Her eyes met Bonnie's for a second, wavered, then fell away.

"Remind me never to have a kid, OK?" she said. "Take it from me—parenthood sucks." She fidgeted with her lock for a moment, taking an extra long time to snap it in place. When she finished, she straightened up and wiped her palms on her khakis. Her eyes were dry but bright, and her lips were pressed tightly together.

"But that's enough of the pity party, OK? We're going to have lots of fun, right?"

"Sure. But then, alas, we'll have to leave my place and go to the dance with Carter and Company."

Jen managed to crack a wan smile.

"You owe me big time for this, Bonnie. I would have loved to go out with Joe. On that triple date thing, I mean."

"I know, I know," Bonnie sighed. "I would have rather done that too. I was just being...oh, I don't know... wimpy?"

"You were being *honourable*!" Jen said, bopping Bonnie on the head with a notebook. "And it's exactly what you would have told one of our blog people to do, don't you think?"

Bonnie could see her point. But privately, she knew that her decision probably had more to do with wishy-washiness than with honour.

SURVIVAL SKILL #6:

ALWAYS EXPECT THE UNEXPECTED.

That evening Jen called Tina from Bonnie's place. She was munching on an apple and surfing the web as she talked.

Suddenly, she bounced a little in her chair.

"…Tina? Gotta dash. Yeah, I promise. By midnight and not a nano-second later. Love to Jules. *Ciao*."

She hit END and called out, "Bonnie! Come check it out!"

Bonnie's heart skipped a beat. She squinted but still couldn't see the screen—she was standing across the room, ironing out the wrinkles from Jen's locker-smushed dress.

"Are you on our blog? Did we finally get another question?"

"Two. We got two new posts!"

"Really?"

"Uh-huh! Unplug that iron, Bonnie. The dress is fine the way it is. Come and look."

Bonnie deked around the ironing board and read.

Dear Bonnie and Jen,

I've got a crush on someone I really shouldn't.
Letting her know would be a really bad idea. But I
can't stop thinking about me and her together. What
should I do?
—Crushed

"Whoa," Bonnie said, "That's not your average
breakfast cereal."

"Keep reading, Bonnie. The next one's no bowl of
Alpha-bits either."

Dear Bonnie and Jen,

I think I'm losing my mind. I never get any sleep
because my younger brother is in a wheelchair now
and he needs lots of help during the night and it
wakes me up. My grades are tanking and I think I'm
about to fail most of my classes. Plus no one pays
any attention to me, not since Bradley Jr. had his
big accident. My folks barely even know I'm there
half the time, so I have no one to turn to for help.
The accident was three whole years ago, but to my
parents, it's like it happened just yesterday, and they
are still totally freaked out. Don't get me wrong—I
feel bad for Bradley Jr.— and for my parents, too.
I feel totally guilty and selfish thinking only about
myself. But still, I'm at the end of my rope. I'm
thinking leaving home might be the way to go but I

have no idea where I would go or what I would do when I got wherever I wound up. I just know I can't take it anymore.

Please help.

—Invisible

Bonnie sank down on the foot of her bed. "Wow."

"Yeah," Jen said. "Can I ever relate to Invisible."

"This *second* one is pretty serious. A lot more serious than Limbo Queen."

"*Uh-huh*. Which means we better be careful what we say."

"The first one's not so hard, though. Don't do it. Period," Bonnie said. "It's wrong."

A crease formed between Jen's eyebrows. "How can you be so sure? You've barely had time to think about it. And we don't know all the facts."

"We don't need *all* the facts," Bonnie said vehemently. "We've got enough. You don't need to be a genius to read between the lines of this one."

Jen shook her head slowly. "I don't know how you do it. How you can always be so, so, *sure* about things. I mean, things aren't always black and white. Sometimes they're grey."

"Or day-glo purple and yellow," Bonnie said, pointing to Jen's party dress. "That dress is so pretty."

Jen just gave Bonnie a stern look. One that meant, 'Don't change the subject.'

Bonnie held up her hands. "OK, I hear you. Everything

is grey from now on. I won't 'jump to conclusions.' And I'll 'look before I leap.' I've been told those things a thousand times, too."

"So maybe you'll listen this time? Anyway, it's time to get dressed. It's almost six. Carter's going to be banging on the door any minute and here I am, still sitting here in my 'pretty kitty' panties."

"I know, I know! It's just that it's hard to concentrate when all I want to do is put together our blog answer."

"Throw me the dress, Bon." Jen stuck her arm out and wiggled her fingers.

Bonnie made a face and flicked the dress at her. It landed squarely on her head.

SURVIVAL SKILL #7:

IT IS NOT NECESSARY TO SAY EVERYTHING YOU THINK.

"Very nice. VER-y nice," Carter said.

Bonnie would have bitten off her own tongue before she acknowledged it, but Carter didn't actually look half bad himself. He was wearing his school's "dress" uniform: a navy blazer and grey trousers with a brilliant white shirt. Gold cufflinks—she figured he'd swiped them from Otto—gleamed at his wrists, and his tasselled loafers shone like mirrors. His normally dishevelled hair looked freshly washed and glossy. And when he smiled that dazzling smile? Well, even Bonnie had to admit to herself that he looked great.

Like a perfect gentleman, Carter pointedly held out one elbow to Jen. Jen's lips twitched. She shyly slipped her hand through the crook of his arm.

Bonnie was just thinking how appearances can be deceiving when Carter crooked his *other* arm. He pointed it expectantly in *her* direction. For *her* to take.

Who did Mr. Suave think he was? James Bond with a girl on each arm?

She almost voiced the wisecrack, but the look on Jen's face stopped her cold.

Jen, Bonnie saw, was enjoying herself.

Bonnie gave her head a private shake. After all that Jen had to put up with at home, Bonnie reckoned she was well overdue for some fun. So for Jen's sake, Bonnie resigned herself to 'being a good sport.'

She took Carter's arm. With some awkward bumpings of hips and a few stepped-on toes, all three of them made it down the stairs together, arm in arm in arm.

Bonnie's mother and stepfather were beaming at the bottom.

"Oh my!" her mother cooed. "Don't you all look swish!"

"Very spiffy indeed," Otto said.

Swish? Spiffy? What are we, air fresheners? Bonnie thought.

Jen thanked them politely. Bonnie just nodded, wishing she could evaporate like a spritz of April Mist.

Bonnie was finally able to extract her arm from Carter's. *Thank god*, she thought. *Embarrassment over.* But it wasn't quite.

Carter was still attached to Jen. He kept her hand in his, raising it up so he was now holding it over her head. Then he kind of pushed and pulled at her to make her do a ballerina twirl.

Bonnie cringed, thinking, *Uh oh, she's gonna punch his lights out.*

But Jennifer didn't punch him.

She didn't yell at him or step on his foot or call him a magna-jerk or a crinoid.

She giggled.

Bonnie's eyes widened. *Did Jen—HER Jen—just giggle? At* Carter?

Bonnie reasoned. Jennifer was wearing three-inch stilettos. Bonnie was positive scientists would eventually prove that the damn things cut off blood flow to the brain.

Bonnie's mother stopped gushing long enough to deliver the usual instructions: Be home by midnight; Call if there is a problem, have fun, etcetera etcetera. Then Carter, Jennifer, and Bonnie were off.

SURVIVAL SKILL #8:

BE POLITE.

Carter had arranged for a cab to take them to the banquet hall. Their first stop, though, was to pick up Carter's friend Dan. Dan was going to be Bonnie's 'date' for the night. It wasn't a date, but even so, Bonnie was so nervous about meeting him that she'd barely eaten all day. Now, as the big moment drew near, her heart was pounding in her ears like a steel drum.

Dan was ready and waiting when the cab pulled up in front of his house. Surprise, surprise: Dan was virtually a Carter clone. Not only was he dressed exactly like him, even down to the shiny polished loafers, but he even had the same brand of blue eyes, the same patented wavy hair (although it was a shade lighter than Carter's), and the same chisel-straight type of nose. He could have come right out of Prep School central casting.

Just great, Bonnie thought. *Two Carters. Shoot me now.*

He squeezed into the car beside Bonnie and reached across her to do some bro' handshake thing with Carter.

Bonnie wished Carter would hurry up and make the introductions so they could get the worst part of the evening over with. But when Carter said, "Dan, this is Bonnie; Bonnie, Dan," Dan barely acknowledged her. He merely grunted and turned his eyes quickly away. He settled stiffly into his seat and stared intently at the passenger headrest in front of him, running his index finger repeatedly around the inside of his shirt collar like it was choking him.

Bonnie's stomach sank. Not that she was *interested* in him or anything. And there was no reason to think he had any interest in her. But shouldn't he at least say *hello* to his 'date?' Shouldn't he even *attempt* to demonstrate basic social skills?

Naturally, if he was Carter's friend, Dan must also hail from Planet Rude—Bonnie had expected that. She still couldn't decide, though, if she should be more mortified than pissed off, or vice-versa. But once her heart had stopped pounding like a tympani, she realized she was simply relieved. If he didn't like her, well, that was one less thing to worry about. The last thing she wanted, after all, was this jerk-friend of Carter's pawing her. Or, as Celia had described so delightfully, sticking his tongue down her throat. But at the same time, if she was honest with herself, Bonnie would have to acknowledge her feelings were hurt. *Was she really so awful that he couldn't even stand to look at her?*

The humiliation made her feel even more ridiculously self-conscious than usual. She couldn't stop angsting about her looks, about her dress riding up her thigh, about her breath. Worst of all, she was sure that if she lifted her arms, they'd release a whuff of sweaty armpit. Talk about mortification!

She tried a little peppy self-talk, telling herself that *she* was just fine, and that *he* was a waste of skin, and not worth another moment of her precious brain space. She told herself she should just ignore him, in the same way he was ignoring her. And she reminded herself again and again that he was completely *irrelevant* as far as she was concerned.

Bonnie scrunched herself into as small a ball as she could. She tried vigilantly not to let any part of her body touch his, but it was an impossible task. She could feel the heat of his thigh burning through the thin silk of her dress, and the smooth fabric of his jacket caressing her bare arm. But she was trapped, unable to pull away. There was simply nowhere to go.

Bonnie stared blindly out the window and wondered how she was going to survive the party without drowning herself—or somebody else—in the punch bowl.

SURVIVAL SKILL #9:

KNOW YOUR ENEMY.

When they arrived at the party, Dan climbed out of the cab first. Still without uttering a word, he offered Bonnie his hand. She gratefully took it—getting out of a car in a dress and heels was a bugger. But once she was up and on her feet, to Bonnie's surprise, Dan didn't let it go. He actually clamped his hand even tighter around hers.

Dan marched at a quickstep into the banquet hall. Bonnie tottered behind him, struggling to keep up in her backless heels. She craned her neck to see if Jen and Carter were following them, but Dan had lost them at the get-go. Bonnie was on her own.

Clearly, Bonnie thought, accepting Carter's invitation had been a huge mistake. How she ever allowed herself to get stuck with this cold fish—or rather, stuck *to* this cold fish—she didn't even know.

Still seemingly oblivious to her presence at the end of his arm, Dan led her toward a cluster of horsy-looking boys. They had commandeered a table close to the loudspeakers. When they reached the table, Dan was greeted by an ear-splitting chorus of "Dan, my man!" and "Looking slick!" As he exchanged fist bumps with his buddies, Bonnie stood awkwardly at his side, feeling like a total jerk.

Dan eventually remembered to make introductions. He fired the names at Bonnie so fast, though, that she couldn't keep track of who was who. It didn't help that all the names sounded like variations of each other: Ty, Taylor, Kyle, Schuyler.

Bonnie was desperate to sit down, but Dan was still clutching her hand in a death-grip. And there weren't any seats anyway—the Centaurs, as Bonnie started thinking of them, had their hooves up on some of the chairs. Others were piled high with jackets and napkins or covered with half-drunk glasses of pop. So Bonnie just shuffled back and forth from one foot to the other, vaguely aware that a blister had started to announce itself on the ball of her big toe. A ring of perspiration, she also knew, was leaving an ever-expanding dark 'collar' on the front of her dress. Nice.

With the sweat dripping inexorably into her bra and the world's fakest smile plastered on her face, Bonnie felt like the Queen of Dorks.

No, she thought, *she was even worse than a dork. She was absolutely hopeless—even more of a stick-in-the-mud than the prep-school girls Celia had mocked.* Bonnie felt herself fading and fading until she was nothing but a black-line drawing, separated from the real, 3-D world of Dan and his Centaur pals by an invisible pane of glass.

SURVIVAL SKILL #10:

KNOW YOUR EMMENTALER FROM YOUR GRUYERE.

After what seemed like an eternity of awkward misery, Dan finally let her hand slip from his. She wriggled her clammy fingers with relief.

At last she could escape.

Bonnie eased away from Dan as unobtrusively as she could. She craned her neck, searching for Jen—or Carter, even—but she couldn't see them.

Bonnie hadn't eaten all afternoon, she had been so nervous. Now, her stomach growled in protest. She glanced around quickly to see if anyone had heard it, but no one was giving her a strange look. She was safe, *so far, anyway.* But Bonnie realized she'd better get something to eat fast, or she'd be totally doomed. Outed as a loser by her own opinionated gut.

She spotted a tall table where a cheese tray was displayed in isolated splendour. She edged closer to it. It looked really good—there were veggies too.

Eat me, they said.

Bonnie grabbed a red pepper strip and a cherry tomato

and gobbled them down, not even bothering with dip.

Right away, she started to feel better. She still couldn't see Jen, but all was not lost; she was quite busy enjoying the company of her *second* best friend, Cheese Tray.

Pathetic as it seemed, Bonnie was starting to have fun.

She was reaching for her third cherry tomato when her eyes happened to fall on the Beautiful Boy.

Now if you have ever in your mind sketched the most perfect-looking dream boy, one that you would have made to order just for yourself if you could, well, Beautiful Boy was him. He was a perfect digital copy of the perfect boy Bonnie had imagined a thousand times. He was tall, but not too tall, with curling dark hair that seemed to frame his face like a picture. And what a face! Clear skin, large, light eyes ringed with thick dark lashes, aquiline nose, full mouth. Just looking at him made the floor drop away under Bonnie's feet—and her stomach drop with it.

Forget that third cherry tomato. Now she had a real mission: to meet the Beautiful Boy.

SURVIVAL SKILL #11:

DON'T LET YOURSELF BE THROWN OFF COURSE AT THE FIRST OBSTACLE.

Bonnie took a deep fortifying breath. With her eyes locked on the Beautiful Boy, she started off after him. Blister be damned.

"Bonbon!"

To her utter annoyance, Carter suddenly surfaced at her side. His breath was warm on her ear.

Figures, she fumed. *I finally come across my ideal guy, and I lose him forever, thanks to Carturd.* She tried to catch another glimpse of the elusive Adonis before he vanished, but no such luck. He was already gone.

Bonnie clenched and unclenched her fists, struggling to keep a firm grip on herself. She didn't have great success. If she could have gotten away with it, she would have smacked Carter over the head with the cheese tray.

Carter, on the other hand, was beaming and gleaming, totally oblivious. "There you are!" he said with delight, shouting to make himself heard over the ear-splitting music. "Let me get you a plate! We wouldn't want you to faint from starvation, now, would we?"

Bonnie tapped her foot. "Where's Jen?"

"On the dance floor with Bobby-O. She sure can shake it."

Bonnie did a double-take. *Jen? Dancing? With someone named Bobby-O? Without Bonnie?* Carter kept on talking as he shepherded her toward the main buffet table. He blathered on about his friends and who was doing what with whom as he piled her plate with food. She tried to stop him, yelling in his ear that she was leaning toward vegetarianism so a rack of ribs wouldn't really go down well, but he either couldn't hear her or just ignored her. The meat mountain on the plate just grew bigger and bigger. Then he ushered Bonnie to an empty table at the far end of the room.

"Here's a nice quiet spot where we can be alone for a few minutes, Bonbon," he said.

She snorted, plunking herself ungracefully in the chair. She slipped off her shoe and gratefully rubbed her throbbing toe.

"Don't you get enough of that with me at home?" she said crossly.

Carter shook his head sadly. "Why do you always do that—rag on me? No, Bonnie, I hardly ever see you at home—let alone *converse* with you. You never let me near you. You always shut yourself away with Jen and shoo me away like a mosquito or something."

Distracted by her painful toe, Bonnie responded without thinking. "Maybe I wouldn't shoo you away if

67

you didn't make yourself so obnoxious all the time."

Carter slammed his hands against the edge of the table. "Oh yeah? I'm obnoxious all the time, am I? Is it obnoxious to bring you to this very nice party?" He waved his arm at the room. "Is it obnoxious to invite you and your little friend and put up with your stupid little games and in-jokes and eye-rolling and insults all the flippin' time?

"Maybe it's you that's obnoxious, did you ever think of that, precious Bonbon? Maybe you should get a life, OK?"

He threw his napkin on the table. It landed right on Meat Mountain, sending barbecue sauce flying. Then he walked away, leaving Bonnie feeling sick to her stomach and very, very confused.

SURVIVAL SKILL #12:

KEEP A FIRM GRIP ON YOUR ROSE-COLOURED GLASSES.

Bonnie left the plate right where it was and went off in a daze to find Jen.

She felt like a worm. No, she felt lower than a worm. Bonnie felt like a parasite on a worm's belly.

Everywhere she looked there were little knots of people looking happy, looking normal, chattering away. She had always believed that those Prep school types were major losers. But now, as she watched them laughing and dancing and munching on chicken wings, she couldn't help wondering, *is it them, or is it me?*

Was Carter actually right? Was it Bonnie that needed to get a life? Granted, she wasn't the most popular girl at Our Lady of Overactive Hormones. But she didn't think it was because she was obnoxious.

But what if Carter was right? What if *he* was normal, and *she* was the one that was out of touch with basic social norms and codes of behaviour? Maybe arm-farting and rude jokes and poor personal grooming were the mainstream, and Bonnie was living in her own deluded backwater? No wonder Dan had no time for her.

Her stomach sank even further.

She wobbled on her heels for a moment as a wave of dizziness and shame swept over her. She steadied herself against one of the tall tables that held a scatter of empty glasses.

Get a grip, she thought. Bonnie suddenly remembered something Celia had once said. Celia had been talking about when she was in high school, before she got her scholarship to the University of Guelph and went off to be brilliant at environmental studies. She had said, "I always felt back then like I was Alice looking through the mirror. Everybody else sort of looked normal, but when I tried to get a closer look at them, they kind of had this pale, double edge, like they weren't really there. Which meant I could never fit in—my edges were just too sharp, my colours too bright. There was always a divide between us.

"I was always doubting myself—is it *them* that's the reflection, or *is it me?* It wasn't until I got to University that I realized why I always felt so out of it. It's because I wasn't on the same wavelength as most of the people I knew in high school. But now I'm surrounded by people more like me. Here, I can be myself. People *get* me."

Bonnie recognized that if someone who didn't know Celia heard her say that, they would figure she was a huge snot or something. But she wasn't. What Celia was was scary smart, off the charts brilliant. She *didn't* fit in with regular people.

Bonnie knew she wasn't as smart as Celia. But still,

she had understood right away what Celia was talking about. Bonnie started thinking that maybe there was more than one way to be like Celia's Alice. After all, Bonnie didn't fit in any more than Celia did. And maybe *that's* what Carter was talking about.

But if Carter was normal, Bonnie thought with a sick twisting of her gut, *then, yeah, I really am a freak...*

"Thank heavens! There you are! I thought I'd lost you forever!" Jen threw her arms around Bonnie's neck, practically strangling her. "Where've you been?"

Bonnie mumbled something about getting some food but Jen wasn't listening. She was saying how much fun she was having on the dance floor and how Bonnie had to go and dance with her because she had asked the DJ to play their all-time favourite song.

Bonnie tried to tell her she wasn't quite up for dancing, but Jen was pushing her from behind and Bonnie was being forced in the direction of the dance floor despite all her best efforts to stay put.

And then the first chords of Green Day's "Holiday" started, and Jen was kicking off her shoes and jumping up and down with her hands on Bonnie's shoulders so she really had no choice but to jump up and down with her.

They were in the thick of the action, grooving to Green Day and Bonnie had almost started to get into it when she noticed that the sweating, gyrating guy about two centimetres from her face was none other than Beautiful Boy.

SURVIVAL SKILL #13:

SOMETIMES YOU JUST GOTTA GO WITH IT.

He smiled.
At Bonnie.

The clouds parted, the sun shone, the orchestra swelled.

She smiled back.

And suddenly she wasn't dancing to "Holiday" with Jen. She was dancing instead with the Beautiful Boy, and he was about as close to her as you could get and still not be touching. So when the song ended, Bonnie wasn't at all surprised that he ran his finger lightly down her arm and took her hand in his while they caught their breath and waited for the next song to start. He was still smiling at her. In fact, he had not stopped smiling at her since that first moment. Bonnie hadn't stopped smiling either.

The next song started and they danced to it, and to the next song, too. Bonnie had no idea what those songs were, other than that they were fast and furious and her heart was racing and soaring all at once. Somewhere in the back of her mind she realized that Jen had left the dance floor. She didn't know with whom. And to be honest, she didn't care.

Again, the music ended, and this time Beautiful Boy gently took Bonnie's other hand and pulled her to him. She could feel his chest rising and falling next to hers. His lips brushed Bonnie's hair and she thought he was asking for her name when the next song, a slow one, started. He folded Bonnie in his arms and they danced. Close.

Too soon, the song stopped, and the DJ team announced they were going to change it up—there were awards to be handed out. They reluctantly pulled apart, but Beautiful Boy was still holding her hands. Bonnie prayed hard that he wouldn't say "Thanks" and disappear out of her life forever.

But he didn't. Instead, he wrapped her in his arms again, and this time when his lips brushed her hair she heard him say, "You are so beautiful. Don't leave me tonight."

She lifted her chin to look into his eyes.

"What is your name?" he whispered.

"Bonnie," she whispered back, as his forehead touched hers. "What's yours?"

"Paolo."

"That sounds Italian," she said. And then felt like a huge moron.

He put his finger to Bonnie's lips. Then he led her off the dance floor, through the wide double doors into the night.

JEN.* <3   12:15AM
WELL??????

b.o.n.n.i.e :)   12:16AM
Wel wat?

JEN.* <3   12:16AM
Wat hapNd? HU iz he? Can't believe u couldn't get a sec to talk all night!

b.o.n.n.i.e :)   12:17AM
His name is Paolo. Hes from Turin Italy. He bordz at Prep H.

JEN.* <3   12:17AM
AND...????

b.o.n.n.i.e :)   12:17AM
And hes AMAZING!!!!!!!

JEN.* <3   12:18AM
I saw U go outside. Did U...?

b.o.n.n.i.e :)   12:18AM
No, he didn't even try to. We just talkd. And talkd & talkd.

b.o.n.n.i.e :)   12:19AM

It waz incredible. Did I say hes AMAZING alreD?

JEN.* <3   12:20AM

That is totalE awesum!!! Im so jelus!!!!

b.o.n.n.i.e :)   12:21AM

U lookd like U were having fun 2.

JEN.* <3   12:21AM

Ya I had a really gr8 time. Did he take ur #?

b.o.n.n.i.e :)   12:22AM

YES! He sez he'll call next week after his exams. Can U come ovR 2morro? I have so much 2 tel U!!!!!

JEN.* <3   12:23AM

Sure. + we have to rite r answers 2 crushed and invisible.

b.o.n.n.i.e :) 12:24AM

O! I completely 4got! Hows 1:30 4 U?

JEN.* <3 12:24AM

Gr8. CU then, lucky duck. Get sum sleep!

b.o.n.n.i.e :) 12:25AM

Yeah rite! Im 2 excited 2 sleep!!!! L8R BF. Luvya.

° Dear Crushed,

You say you have the hots for someone you "shouldn't." That tells me you already know what you should and should not do. So why are you asking us?

 • He's asking us, Bonnie, because life isn't always so black and white.

 ° I dunno about that. Right and wrong are pretty black and white to me.

 • Crushed, you and I both have a problem here. Bonnie doesn't get shades of grey.
You and I, however, apparently know better. For example, I can see that there are several possible shades right there in your question. What do you mean by "should" after all? Why *shouldn't* you have a crush on this person? Because they "belong" to someone else? Because you've decided you're not the type to have a crush? Because they are different from the kind of person you expected to ever fall for?

 ° I think you're reading too much into this. He says he shouldn't be thinking about this person. Let's assume that he's talking about somebody out of bounds. If it was more complicated than that he would have said, right?

 • Maybe.

○ Definitely. So let's take a stab at this. If we're wrong, Crushed, you write back and straighten us out, OK?

So let's say he's discovered that he can't stop thinking about, say, his girlfriend's best friend. That fits his story.

 • Yup. And it would definitely be a no-no. The RULES OF ROMANCE say it right there at the top of the scroll: Thou Shalt Not Make Goo-goo Eyes at Your Sweetie's Best Friend. Or vice-versa.

 ○ Crushed knows this. The problem is that he's still thinking…and thinking…and thinking…and it's driving him mental.

 • Welcome to my Universe, Crushed! I've been mental for years! At least, since I met Bonnie.

 ○ Thanks, BF. Did I happen to mention I have some arsenic cola for you in the fridge?

 • I'm thinking that Crushed's real question is, how can he deal with his temptation so that no one gets hurt?

 ○ Other than moving to a monastery in France?

• Let's try and offer him a solution that won't interfere quite so much with his future career options.

 ○ Staying way far away from Miss Trouble would be my first bit of advice. No cozy get-togethers doing homework. No frantically working late, side by side, on the school paper. No long walks home from school when you accidentally-on-purpose miss the last bus.

 • Good point, Bonnie. Out of sight, out of mind and all that.

 ○ Besides, it's hard to cheat with someone if you never get the chance to, you know, actually be in the same room with them.

 • Here's my advice: Make a list of what the consequences would be if you actually did slip up. "Girlfriend will dismember me; will lose friendship of both girls; will feel like a tool if she laughs at me, etc." Post the list in your room and look at it whenever you feel yourself starting to daydream about Dragonlady again. And wear a rubber band on your wrist to remind you of the list whenever you're out of the house.

 ○ Two rubber bands if you'll be in temptation's way, like at school or at a party where this girl is gonna be.

• Anyway, be strong. As bad as you think you'll feel now, you'll feel worse if you go against your instincts and have to live with a guilty conscience.

 ○ Don't ask Jen how she knows this. She's not telling. Me neither. Uh-uh. Lips sealed with krazy glue.

 • Unfortunately Bonnie did not get krazy glue on her keyboard and she can still type *evilly glaring across room at Bonnie*.

Let's just say there have been things I have done that I am not entirely proud of. But who hasn't? Remember that saying? "Let she who is without sin throw the first stone…"

I think the idea is that we are all supposed to learn from our mistakes *throwing beanie octopus at Bonnie's head*. And I've learned this: If you're not going to like waking up with yourself after you've done something, you better not do it. Because whatever good feeling you get out of doing the bad thing (staying longer at the fun party, getting to be with that girl, bringing home the A on the test you cheated on) doesn't last as long as the rotten feeling that comes along with it.

You can trust me on this one—or find out the hard way. It's your call, Crushed. But for my money, I'm with Bonnie. Steer clear, OK?

° But you know, Crushed, whatever you wind up doing, even if you blow it and wind up regretting it, You will survive!!

Keep bringing us the updates,
Jen and Bonnie

• Dear Invisible,

Boy, do I ever relate to what you are saying,
Invisible! I, like you, never get any sleep. My baby
sister is 30 months old, and it has been pretty tough
to have a life since the day she came home from the
hospital. Don't get me wrong—she's cute as a bug
and I love her to death—but life with an infant is not
for wimps.
My dad died just before Julia was born, so it's just
my mom and me to look after the baby. The kid part
of me doesn't get much play time. I have to help
around the house too much. Sometimes, I *wish* I
were invisible!!!!

 ○ I can relate, too. I have two little brothers. (Half-
brothers, really.) Connor is 4 and Colin is 2. They
don't live with me, they live with my dad and his
new wife. So I don't have the problem of being
kept up at night like you, but I do know what it
feels like to be left out. Joe (that's my real brother)
described us (my dad's first family) as "last season's
coolest fashions—marked down to 70% off on the
'everything must go!' clearance rack", while Connor
and Colin (the new kids) are this year's hot styles.
Yeah, Joe's just a little bitter.

 • Leaving home, however, is definitely NOT the
solution. If you think you feel invisible now, do you

have any idea how invisible you'd become once you were a street kid?

 ○ My mom does some volunteer work with an agency that helps homeless people. She meets a lot of street kids. She tells me about them sometimes, and believe me, from what I've heard, you don't want to be one. *shudders* No matter how bad you think things are now, being out there is much, much worse.

 • We hear you though. You can't keep going on like this. You feel like you've got a really bad situation at home and you are sinking fast. You need to get some help ASAP. Not that I mean to get all preachy on you or anything.

 ○ I hope this doesn't sound really lame, but is there anyone at school you can talk to? A teacher or a guidance counselor?

 • I called Kids Help Phone a couple of times when things got rough for me, back in the bad old days when my mom was having some problems. They were really helpful.

 ○ You called KH? I didn't know that.

 • Shocking but true—I don't tell you everything!!!!!!

I wish you had. There were times I probably could have used the number too.

Invisible, pay attention: You are not invisible anymore, OK? We know you are out there, and we know things are really not great for you right now. We care what happens to you.
But we can only do so much, right? You are going to have to take the next teensy step yourself. Please— talk to someone. Today. Then let us know what happens. We really, really want to know you are OK.

And remember, no matter what happens:
You will survive!!!

With X-Ray Glasses, the better to see you with,

Jen and Bonnie

SURVIVAL SKILL #14:

IN TIMES OF CRISIS, DRINK PLENTY OF STRONG TEA.

Bonnie's cell phone rang with a disgustingly loud chirp right next to her ear. She pried open one eye to check the clock. It was Sunday, and it was morning, but barely. Bonnie rolled over and pulled the pillow over her head.

The phone chirped again.

She tried to ignore it and stay immersed in her dream. Paolo was in it—what more was there to say?

The phone stopped chirping for a micro-second, then started again. Bonnie began to wonder whether she had been sane the day she had picked that ring tone for her phone. It was hideous. It was *obnoxious*.

She stuck her hand out. It scrabbled around on the nightstand like a drunken lobster until its clumsy pincers closed on its prey.

She hit TALK.

"Yeah?" she mumbled as she brought the phone to her ear.

Jen said, "Tina didn't come home last night."

"Oh my God," Bonnie said, instantly wide awake.

"When I got home from your place, there were no lights on or anything. Tina usually leaves the hall light on for me when I'm out. I called out softly to let her know I was home, but, you know, not loud enough to wake Julia. I didn't get an answer. So I looked in her room. Tina wasn't there. I then went in to check on Julia and she wasn't in her crib. I almost freaked.

"I called the babysitter right away. Yeah, Julia was there. Tina hadn't come to get her at three like she always did. Mrs. Serakis was worried sick. She'd even called the hospitals looking for her."

"Jen," Bonnie said, "why didn't you call me right away? You can't stay there by yourself! Lemme wake up Mom. We'll be right there."

"Wait! Stop, Bonnie. Tina's OK. She's back now."

Bonnie knew what was coming next. She'd been there before for this next part.

"What happened, Jen?"

"She rolled in about a half an hour ago."

"Is she—?"

"As a skunk."

Bonnie exhaled, a slow, long breath. It wasn't the first time that Tina had come home drunk. But it had been a while since the last time, and Jen had started hoping that maybe it wouldn't happen again. So that's why Jen hadn't called her or the cops the second she'd discovered Tina wasn't home. She was pretty sure Tina would be home in her own sweet time. And she was right.

86

"Then what happened?" Bonnie prodded.

"Oh, the usual. I helped her out of her stinky clothes and gave her a couple of large glasses of water and some Advils and put her to bed. Then I called the babysitter to tell her that Mom was OK—just a misunderstanding. And that I'd come and get Julia at eight."

"Bring Julia over here, Jen."

"I was hoping you'd suggest that. If you hadn't, I would have asked myself."

"It'll be OK."

"Right. And Lady Gaga's the Tooth Fairy." There was a long pause. "I'm sorry I woke you, Bon. I couldn't wait any longer."

"'Course not, Jen. I love you, you know."

"Yeah, I know. Thanks. I love you, too."

I am completely and totally worried about
Jennifer. She's never really got it back
together 100% since her dad died two and a
half years ago. And who could blame her
after what happened?

Tina's drinking was what started it. She
had been drinking on and off for years, but
what drove Jen's dad mental was that she
was still drinking even after she got pregnant.
They had a huge fight. They had lots of
fights, but according to Jen, this one went
nuclear. In the end, Jen's dad said there was
no way he was going to stay with a drunk
any longer and watch her give their baby fetal
alcohol syndrome.

Tina screamed back at him, calling him
awful names (Jen wouldn't tell me what)
and told him she was going to have the
baby, with or without him, and he screamed
back, fine, then without him it was, and
he stormed out of there in his 4 x4, tires
squealing.

Wrapped the truck around a tree. End of
story.

After he died, well, you can only imagine
how awful things were in Jen's house.

It's not like Tina hasn't tried her best
to be a good mom, both to Jen and Julia.

But how on earth could anybody pull it together—anybody!—after what had happened? I mean, of course she felt guilty as all get-out. Like it was her fault he went speeding out of there and crashed the truck. And then, a few months later Tina had this new kid to look after, and everybody knows how hard new babies are to care for.

Tina stopped drinking after the accident—cold turkey—but couldn't stick it, so after a few weeks, Jen was back to looking for hidden bottles of booze and making sure Julia was clean and fed and taken to the sitter at the right time. Tina, though, didn't give up—she finally got sober on Julia's first birthday, and hadn't had a drink since. Or so she says. But every single day of the last one and a half years, Jen has been watching Tina like an eagle. It's almost like Jen has become the mom, and Tina's the troubled teen on probation.

So who is there to look after Jen?

Me.

But this is way out of my league. I mean, my dad moved out, and that sucked, but he didn't die.

He's told me a million billion times in that deep, ultra-serious tone, "I left the marriage, not you," and he's tried to show

89

me he means it. OK, so he's sometimes a phony, but at least he's around. And I guess even though I still get really mad at him for leaving us and marrying Katie, I do know deep down he does really love me.

And yeah, sometimes Mom gets on my nerves with all her speechifying and do-gooding and Honesty is the Best Policy righteousness. But she's a great mom. She's always been there. If there were a hurricane and an earthquake and an alien invasion all happening at the same time, she would still drive up in her van, on time, to pick me up from wherever I needed picking up from. She always made sure we had three squares a day, clean clothes, and fresh toilet paper on the roller thingy. I have never for one second had to wonder if she was out drinking or if she'd make it home or if she'd hurt me when she's had one too many.

But Jen, now that's another story all together. This isn't little kid stuff. It's real. We're not talking broken crayons and torn Valentines and getting chosen last for dodge ball. We're talking Children's Aid and Legal Custody and Rehab.

Bottom line: If Tina's not able to look after Jen and Julia, she may lose them.

And if that happens, then I may lose Jen.

SURVIVAL SKILL #15:

CALL IN REINFORCEMENTS AS THE SITUATION DEMANDS.

Bonnie and her mother barely exchanged two words during the car ride to Jen's house. Bonnie knew her mother was really worried, not only about Jen and Julia, but about Tina too.

Jen was sitting on the front steps when they pulled up. Bonnie threw open the van door and ran to her. She sat down beside her and hugged her tight. Jennifer was struggling hard not to cry, but her chest was heaving and her shoulders were shaking.

"Thanks for coming, Mrs. Bartels...I mean, um, Mrs. Molnar..."

Bonnie's mom sat down on Jen's right. She patted Jennifer on the back and laughed a little. "Sometimes I don't know what to call myself either. Don't worry about it.

"Why don't we go inside? We can talk about things better if we get more comfortable."

Bonnie could tell Jen didn't want to go back inside, but she let out a deep sigh, got to her feet and allowed herself to be steered back through the door and into the kitchen.

There was a fresh pot of coffee on the counter. Jen began to busy herself at the sink, wiping up non-existent water spots.

Bonnie's mom took both of Jen's shoulders and gently turned her so that she and Jen were eye to eye. She gave Jen her deep searching look. "Are you really OK, Jennifer?"

Jen glanced away. She was wringing the J-cloth in her hands. "Yes. I mean, no. I'm angry and I'm tired and I'm worried, too. But I *am* OK, really. I'll just feel a lot better once I have Julia with me."

Mrs. Molnar nodded, "Of course. Perfectly understandable. Here's what I suggest: I'll go in and check on Tina. I don't want anything to happen to her while she's sleeping it off. You two girls go to the sitter's and bring Julia back home. I'll start packing some of the things we'll need to have both of you stay at our house for a few days."

"I don't want to come back here again," Jen said, crossing her arms. "Tina will be fine."

"I'm sure she'll be fine, too, Jennifer," said Mrs. Molnar. "I just want to make sure she's all right and doesn't throw up and choke."

Jennifer visibly recoiled. "Tina's never thrown up, ever, from drinking. Really—she's fine. Let's just go."

"She may never have done it before, but things are different now. You said your mom hasn't had a drink in

92

over a year. That's a long time. Her tolerance for alcohol may have changed. We just don't know how this drinking binge will affect her. Look, I'll stay here for a bit. You said the sitter's expecting you by eight. So it's a quarter to already. Go get Julia. Don't worry. I'll be right here when you get back. We won't have to stay long."

Jennifer's eyes welled up with tears and they started spilling over. "I'm so sorry, Mrs. Molnar."

She pulled Jennifer to her and hugged her tight. "You have nothing to be sorry for. Now come on, wipe away those tears. Julia's waiting for you."

Bonnie? Jen?

You there?

—Crushed

SURVIVAL SKILL #16:

MAINTAIN AN EMERGENCY FUND.

Bonnie's mom asked Jen if she needed any money to pay the babysitter.

Jen said, "Tina always keeps some cash in the house in case of an emergency. I always made it my business to know exactly where she hid it. Just in case of, well, an emergency of my own." She twisted her face wryly. "I guess this qualifies." She waved her hand in the direction of Tina's room. Then she disappeared into the back of the house. When she returned, she was stuffing a wad of twenties into her jeans.

Bonnie accompanied Jennifer to the babysitter's house, three blocks away. Through the screen door, they could see Julia scampering around the living room with a stuffed hobby-horse under one arm and a red stuffed dog under the other.

As soon as Julia caught sight of Jen, she dropped both toys and ran screaming to the door.

"Jen-eeeeee! Up! Up!" she screeched, holding her arms out and jumping like a bean. Jen opened the screen door, scooped Julia up, and squeezed her tight.

The babysitter was a middle-aged lady with kind eyes. She was wiping her hands on a kitchen towel as she came to the door.

"Is everything OK at home?" she asked Jen. "If there's a problem, I'm happy to keep Julia. She's a delight, you know."

"Thanks, Mrs. Serakis. Everything's fine. It was just a communication mix-up. My mom's home now, and she asked me to tell you how very sorry she is for inconveniencing you. She gave me this for you." Jen put the wad of cash in Mrs. Serakis's hand. "There's extra there. For your trouble."

Mrs. Serakis's eyes narrowed as she took the money from Jen. Bonnie could tell she didn't believe that everything was OK, but she didn't want to pry. In the end, she just nodded and took the money.

"I've got Julia's gear ready to go," she said. She unhooked a diaper bag from behind the door.

"Give Yaya a kiss," Jen instructed Julia as she hoisted the toddler up and settled her onto her hip. Julia puckered up and left a slobbery mark on Mrs. Serakis's cheek. She waved her chubby fist and said, "Bye-bye, Yaya."

"Bye to you too, Julia dear. I'll see you tomorrow and we'll eat pancakes together, OK? You love pancakes, don't you, my little pancake goblin?"

"Num num, pan-take!" Julia repeated excitedly.

The whole walk back, Julia kept cooing, "Num num,

pan-take! Num num, pan-take!" Jen, in return, hugged her little sister tighter and cooed into her ear, "Does Julia love pancakes? We'll have to have some pancakes then!"

As the two sisters were absorbed in each other, Bonnie let her mind drift—right into a daydream about Paolo. Even throughout the drama of the past few hours, she had barely stopped thinking about him. It was as if, somewhere in the back of her mind, she was running a continuous film loop of Paolo and herself dancing together.

Bonnie allowed her steps to grow slower and slower until she trailed several steps behind Jen and Julia. She let her mind rewind, replaying every single second of Friday evening, savo,ring each one. She lingered longest over the moment when he had pressed his forehead to hers and said, "I must see you again…"

She wondered if she'd be able to stand it, waiting for him to call. Patience was not exactly her strong point. *What would their next "date" be like? Would he kiss her? Would she even like him to kiss her?* The idea was kind of scary. After all, this was no ordinary Toronto boy. This was an Italian. A *gorgeous* Italian. He'd probably kissed hundreds of girls. *What if she messed up? What if he didn't like her that much the next time they saw each other?* Before Bonnie could work herself into a full-blown anxiety attack, though, they arrived back at Jen's place. Bonnie's mother met them at the door.

"I packed up some of Julia's clothes, some toys, and a box of diapers. Jen, could you check and see what else she'll need to stay with us for a week or so? Bonnie, can you load the porta-crib and high chair into the van, please?"

"How's Tina?" Jen asked.

"She's OK," Mrs. Molnar said, her tone business-like. "I was able to wake her up. She drank a glass of water, and went to the bathroom. She's going to have a crashing headache today. We can leave whenever we're ready. She'll call us later.

"Do you want to go in and talk to her before we go, Jennifer?"

"No," Jen stated flatly. She abruptly put Julia on the floor, turned on her heel, and headed towards the nursery.

Bonnie's mom sighed. She put her arm around Bonnie's shoulder. "This is a very difficult day for her," she said. "You're being a good friend."

Bonnie leaned her head against her. "And you're being a great mom. Thanks for everything—you're the best."

SURVIVAL SKILL #17:

STAY CALM AND CARRY ON.

Bonnie and Jennifer hung out in Bonnie's room the rest of the day. Jen didn't talk much. She just curled up in a ball on Bonnie's bed, chewing on her bottom lip. Bonnie wished that she would cry or talk or scream or do something other than just lie there in suspended animation. She felt about as useful as baby Julia, who was asleep and oblivious in her porta-crib at the foot of the bed.

It was around six o'clock when her Mom called up the stairs, "Dinner's ready!"

"Jen, let's go get something to eat."

Jennifer sat up, yawned, and rubbed her face.

"I don't feel hungry. I actually feel kind of sick. But I guess I should eat something…"

"You'll probably feel better if you do."

"I don't think I want to eat dinner with your family, though. I can't handle everybody being all nicey-nicey to me right now."

"How about if I bring up a tray of something?"

"Would you?" Jen said. "You don't think your folks would mind?"

"Naah…they'll understand. Two dinner specials, coming right up. Delivery in thirty minutes or it's free."

Bonnie went down to the kitchen and dished up two plates of chicken paprikash and rice. Then she stepped out onto the back porch where her mom kept some flower pots filled with pansies. She made a little bouquet and put it in a vase on Jen's tray. She threw a white towel over her arm and carried everything up.

"Dinner is served," Bonnie said in her dopiest French accent.

"Thanks for this," Jen said, tapping the pansies to make their heads bob prettily. "The chicken smells good—I must be hungry after all."

They both scooched back on the bed so they could lean comfortably against the wall. Side by side, with their trays on their laps, they began to eat.

"This is really yummy," Jen said. "At home, we haven't had anything cooked from scratch in a while. Tina usually gets home too late and I'm hopeless at cooking. If it doesn't come in a box or go into the microwave, it's beyond me."

She took another bite and savoured it with her eyes closed. "My dad was a good cook. He used to make homemade pasta and real Bolognese sauce. And soup—terrific pea soup. I miss that soup."

"I bet you could learn to make it. I don't think soup is that hard," Bonnie said between bites.

Jen gave her a twisted smile. "It wouldn't taste the same, though. It wouldn't be made by him, ya know? He cooked with love. I know that sounds pretty stupid. But it's the truth—he loved us. A lot."

Bonnie put her hand on Jen's. "Yeah. He did," she said.

"But then, I think, if he loved me so damn much, how could he have stormed out that night like that? I mean, I know he didn't plan on getting himself killed, but still. He had just said he was leaving and wasn't coming back. How could he? Yeah, he was pissed at Tina, but what about me? Didn't he think about me?"

"You know he didn't really mean it, Jen. He was just mad. He would have cooled off and been back in a few hours."

"Well, I guess I'll never really know. I'll always just… wonder." Jen heaved a deep sigh. "Down deep, if I'm honest with myself, I keep thinking he's going to come back. And if he did… Well, everything would be OK. I pretend, every single day, lying to myself, just so I can get up every morning. That's so freaking lame, isn't it?"

Bonnie edged closer to Jen so their shoulders were touching.

"No," she said. "I'm no better. I pretend all the time too. When I'm lying in bed at night, I close my eyes and I sort of just *will* everything that's happened these last five years away. *Poof!* Carter and Otto don't exist. *Poof!* Connor and Colin—never born. Then all I'd have to do is slip out of bed and go into Mom's and Dad's bedroom. And there would be: Dad, just like always, remote in one hand and the newspaper in the other, his glasses practically falling off his nose so he could watch the sports and read the op-ed pages at the same time."

Bonnie felt the tears start sliding down her cheeks.

Jen's hand crept into hers.

"I still have an old shirt of my dad's," Jen offered. "If I concentrate, I can sometimes still get a faint wisp of his smell from it. When I feel really lonely, I slip it inside my pillow case so I can have 'him' with me all night."

"I have one of my dad's shirts, too. *I* sometimes wear it to sleep."

Jen tilted her head so it rested against Bonnie's. Her voice cracking, she said, "Man, we are so pathetic."

"I dunno. We're human is more like it," Bonnie said, wiping her eyes. "I guess this is one of those 'if it doesn't kill you, it makes you stronger moments,' eh?"

"I hope so. I'm not feeling like I'm getting any stronger just yet, though."

"But you will survive this. We both will."

"Sure we will."

Evening began to draw shadows around them. Jen wiped her eyes and nudged Bonnie with her shoulder. "Look at you crying. You're such a jerk."

"Takes one to know one," Bonnie said, nudging her back.

They sat like that for a while, just leaning against each other and holding each other's hands in the dark.

After what seemed like a very long while, Jen whispered, "What do you think is going to happen now? I'm so scared."

"I'll bet," Bonnie whispered back.

Jen squeezed her hand. "Crazy as it sounds, Tina's

the one I could always rely on. She never gave up on us, not for a second. Even with all her problems, she never stormed out. She stayed. Too drunk to move, maybe, but she was *there. Always.* Even with all her problems, she stayed. But now, I can't count on Tina. I can't count on anything."

"Yes, you can," Bonnie said. "You've got me, Jen. And I promise, you can always count on me."

Dear Bonnie and Jen,

The dog ate my homework. Really. What do I tell my teacher?

—Sadface Puppy

 o Dear Sadface Puppy,
That's quite the tail.

 • Doggone awful too.

 o But we believe you. We know truth can be stranger than fiction.

 • And dogs can be stranger than weimeraners.

 o Weimeraners ARE dogs, Jen.

 • Really? I didn't know that!!! <IRONY DUH>

 o Here's our completely canine-worthy advice: Truth is the best policy.

 • Even if it is stranger than fiction.

○ So tell your teacher that the dog ate your homework, and that since you know how ridiculous this sounds, that you are prepared to do *double* homework to make up for the missing paperwork.

 • You might say we even 'double-dog dare you' to do this.

 ○ But there's a good reason to take our suggestion. You see, teachers get really upset when kids lie to them, especially when the fibbers are trying to get out of doing some work. But if you own up, AND take responsibility by offering to do extra work, what can your teacher do other than say 'OK'?

 • Well, maybe they can do something other than say OK, but YOU will have done the RIGHT THING, and then you can deal with whatever happens from a place of strength.

 ○ Right, not from the Doghouse.

 • So, Step 1: Don't go barking up the wrong tree by making up another excuse. Step 2: throw your teacher a bone, and Step 3: you'll end up as top dog!

 ○ And remember, whatever happens, you will survive!
Psst: we're cheerfully wagging our tails at ya!
Bonnie and Jen

Sunday night

I'm writing this while sitting at my desk in one corner of the den while Jen and Tina are having a heart to heart in my bedroom. Tina asked me to stay but I told her I had some schoolwork to do. And that's what I'm doing now, my "schoolwork," ha ha.

Here's what happened: At about 8 o'clock, the doorbell rang. Jen practically froze, with that deer-in-the-headlights look on her face.

I could hear my mom's heels clicking across the front hall, the door opening, and then a woman's voice: Tina.

"Oh man," Jen said. "I SO do not want to talk to her. And I am definitely not going home with her. And I'm not letting her take Julia either."

I told Jen not to worry, and reminded her about how my mom said she'd have a word with Tina first, to let her know that Jen would be staying with us for a few days.

And then I said that it wasn't like Tina didn't know she screwed up. And that since she said she was determined to stay sober, Jen should give her another chance. But Jen was adamant. She said that in her opinion Tina had really, really blown it. And then she started to cry. Those big, fat honking sobs that make you feel awfuller than before you started. She choked them back and said, "You mean I should give her a chance to soften me up with her pitiful excuses? See if she has any different ones now? I thought I heard every one of them already, but I could be wrong."

Then Jen told me what she was really afraid of: that they don't let kids under sixteen stay with parents who can't look after them. And if a parent leaves kids unsupervised overnight, that's a real no-no. Jen said she was scared that Children's Aid will put her and Julia in care as soon as they hear that Tina didn't come home one night. No ifs, ands, or buts.

I told her she was jumping to conclusions, but I admit it, the idea that J and J could be taken away scares the bejeezus out of me, too. So I just reminded her that no one was going to tell Children's Aid to come and get them because there wasn't anyone who knew anything except us.

But then she reminded me that Mrs. Serakis knew, too.

I said Mrs. Serakis wouldn't say anything.

Your mom might, she said.

No frigging way, I told her.

Jen said she hoped I was right because she didn't think she could cope if she got

sent to a foster home or a group home or
something like that. She said she couldn't
stand not having Julia with her, or letting
Julia get adopted, even. She said she'd have
to find her and run away with her. She was
really scaring me so I told her to stop it
RIGHT THIS INSTANT. And that's when
we heard Tina's knock on my bedroom door.

Jen didn't want me to let her in but of
course I had to. So Tina came in, looking
all yellowy and awful. She checked on Julia,
sleeping in the porta-crib, and then started
apologizing to Jen. That's when I decided to
make my exit—it was pretty awkward standing
there during their mother-daughter moment.
So I told her I had homework and got the
heck outta there.

So now Jen and Tina are probably having
a lovefest in my room and I'm over here in
a corner of the den, not sure how I feel
about the whole thing. I feel bad for Tina,
and bad for Jen, but something just does not
sit right with me about this whole situation.

And really, I don't want to be part of it.
Of course I want to help Jen and be there
for her, but this is all just too much for
me! I just want to be able to sink into my
much-more-pleasant thoughts about PAOLO
and not have to worry about Children's Aid

and AA and stuff like that.

All I really want to do is think about
PAOLO........

Paolo

Paolo

Paolo

Paolo

Paolo!!!!!

SURVIVAL SKILL #18:

DON'T PUT THE CART BEFORE THE HORSE. WHATEVER THAT MEANS.

Bonnie's mom was sitting at the kitchen table.

"Well, this has been one seriously bad day," Bonnie said, sitting down heavily across from her.

"It's been a tough one, all right. Do you want something? A cool drink? Or some tea? I've got the kettle going already. I can make you some chamomile."

"What are we going to do?" Bonnie asked.

Her mother began making the tea.

"That's a good question, dear," she said from near the stove. "A lot of it will depend on Tina. If she's serious about doing the right thing, she'll get some help and we can nip this thing in the bud. She really shouldn't have tried to go it alone. It's amazing she made it as long as she did.

"She told me a little bit about herself before she went upstairs," her mom continued, setting a mug of steaming chamomile tea and a plate of butter cookies in front of Bonnie. "I think that both she and Jen could use some family therapy. And Tina needs to get some round the

110

clock support. I can help her get to the right people, but she has to want to do it. If she won't, well, there's not much anyone can do for her."

"But what will happen if she can't cut it?" Bonnie asked, and then told her mom what Jen had said about having to go into Care and being separated from Julia.

"Let's not put the cart before the horse, shall we?" her mom said, patting Bonnie's hand. "Right now, Julia and Jen are staying here. Tina has already agreed. She's going to take a few days to think about what to do. She knows she made a big mistake, and she needs to sort herself out. In the meantime, we'll try and keep things as normal as possible for both girls. We'll take Julia to her sitter every day, and Jen will go to school with you. And speaking of you and Jen, how did the two of you enjoy the party on Friday?"

"We...e...l...l...l..." Bonnie started to say, a warm glow suffusing her entire body. "You see I met this g—"

Carter sauntered into the kitchen. His hand was up his shirt and he was scratching his belly.

Bonnie's mouth snapped shut in mid-word. She turned her face to the wall so her mom wouldn't see the expression of disgust that she was certain it wore.

"Hey, it's Babe-a-licious One and Babe-a-licious Two," he said. "Is this a 'gals only' coffee klatsch, or can I hang with you while I grab a snack?"

Without waiting for an answer, he pulled the milk and a leftover square of pound cake from the fridge. He put them in front of Bonnie, then grabbed some forks and knives from the drawer and tossed them onto the table with a clatter. "You ladies want plates?"

"Thank you, dear," Mrs. Molnar said.

Bonnie gave her mother a despairing look. Why did she have to practically welcome him into their private conversation with open arms?

"Everything OK?" He scooped a giant forkful of cake into his mouth, then swigged a gulp of milk directly from the jug.

Ick, thought Bonnie. Ick. Ick. Ick.

"When I checked in your room for you just now," he said through a sticky blob of cake, "I found Jenny in this deep powwow with someone—is that her mum? Both of them are crying like they're on Oprah or something."

"That is Jennifer's mother, dear. They had a bit of a problem today. Bonnie went over to help. Jennifer and her sister will be staying with us for a few days until they get things sorted out."

Carter nodded, chewed, and swallowed. "Cool. Lemme know if I can help, Bonbon." He reached for the milk. "You know I'd do anything for Jen," he said with a wink.

Bonnie rolled her eyes. Her mother shot her a warning look.

Bonnie said sullenly, "OK, Carter. Will do." Then she shot her mother a look back as if to say, *There! You satisfied?*

"Man, that was what the doctor ordered," Carter said, rubbing his stomach. He suppressed a belch. "I'm going down to the basement to work out. See if I can bench press 150. Wanna spot me, Bonbon?"

Her mother's eyes bored into Bonnie. To Bonnie, they felt like red-hot lasers, beaming the message, *"Be nice, or else..."*

"Maybe next time," Bonnie mumbled. *Yeah right. In your dreams, scuzzball.* Once he was gone, Mrs. Molnar said, "I don't know why you are so hard on him, Bonnie. He really is a sweet boy."

Bonnie practically snorted her tea out her nose. "I'm sure that's what Mrs. Dracula said."

"Really, dear. You can be so *cold* sometimes. I'd better go—before I catch a chill."

Bonnie was left sitting alone at the kitchen table, bewildered.

Have I just been dissed—by my own mother?

SURVIVAL SKILL #19:

THINGS ARE NOT ALWAYS WHAT THEY SEEM.

Bonnie glanced over her shoulder at Jen. She was asleep, finally, on the trundle bed. Julia was snoring lightly in her little crib.

Bonnie was wired, though. Her brain felt like it had electrodes implanted in it. They kept jolting her with panicky little blips. She was definitely what her mom would describe as "out of sorts."

Which was why Bonnie was online at two o'clock in the morning, wide awake and chewing on the ends of her hair. She was surfing the web, trying both to distract herself and to wear herself out in what seemed like a futile effort to still her overactive brain.

Surely Jen won't mind if I take a quick peek at the blog without her, thought Bonnie, after giving up on YouTube. And that's when Bonnie discovered Crushed's latest message.

Dear Bonnie and Jen,

I can't exactly avoid her. We're sort of "housemates."

—Crushed

Crushed's words seemed to present a challenge to Bonnie, as if he were saying, *Go ahead—see if you can tell me what to do now, smartypants.*

Bonnie considered the matter. Would Jen be mad at her if she answered Crushed on her own? They had never said outright that they would only post advice together. It was kind of understood, though. But that was before the whole shlemazzle had happened with Tina. *Why would Jen even care now about Crushed? She had enough on her own plate.*

The cursor blinked at Bonnie, needling her to type something.

She put her fingers on the keyboard. The keys felt warm to her touch, smooth and familiar. Comforting.

 ○ And I suppose finding another place to live is out of the question?

 ⋗ Kewl! You're there! This is awesome. What are you doing up?

 ○ Can't sleep. You?

⋙Me neither. To answer your q, moving out would mean going back to live with my mom. And she's insane. Really. Like she should be committed, but she won't sign herself in. Living with her would be even worse.

 ○ That sounds pretty awful. So you're living with your dad's new family then? A so-called blended family, right?

 ⋙Yup.

 ○ I prefer to think of it as a blend*er* family. Totally mixed up. I've got one too.

 ⋙Yeah, I know. That's what you put in your first post. I figured you might have a good grasp of my situation…

It's like this: My housemate is actually my new step-sister. Last year, my dad introduces us, saying, "This is gonna be your new sister and I'm like, 'Whoa! She's a major babe!' What a loser I am, eh?

 ○ Usually kids hate their new step-sibs.

 ⋙I know. A lot of my friends do. I don't really get why, though. It's not their fault their families got screwed up. They're in the same boat as we are, right?

○ I don't think I'm in the same boat with my step-
brother. I'm not even on the same planet as him.

 ⧐ Why do you say that, Bonnie?

 ○ We're just different, that's all.

 ⧐ Different is good. That's why I'm in the mess I'm
in. She's different from all the other fakey-phony girls
I know. My step-sis is totally cool. She's real, you
know what I mean?

 ○ Maybe she just seems that way because you know
her better than you know other girls. Maybe if you
lived in the same house with other girls, you'd get to
see them without their party faces, too.

 ⧐ Maybe, but I don't think so. She's special, I'm
telling you. And believe me, I know a good thing
when I see it, Bonnie. I'm not a dope. Even if that's
what you're thinking.

 ○ I don't think you're a dope. But you're right,
Crushed. Acting on your feelings would be a
'crushing' mistake. (Sorry—bad pun.) I still say you
should keep your feelings under wraps. They're
probably not "real" anyway. Just a reaction to being
all messed up and angry and stuff.

If you stop and think about it, it's actually quite a brilliant way to get back at your mom and dad and everybody for blowing your family to smithereens. A nice little act of revenge. With your little crush, you get to blow up your new family—*kaBOOM*.

There was a long pause before Crushed's next message appeared.

 ➢ I guess you're right. I'm just an angry messed up jerk with revenge in my heart. I couldn't possibly have genuine feelings for a special person.
I better go. Good night, B.

 ○ Wait, C! I think that might have come out wrong! C? Are you there?

I'm sorry. That was a stupid thing to say.

Good night, C.
Sleep tight.

Bonnie watched and waited for a few minutes, but the screen stayed blank. Crushed had logged off. Bonnie was alone.

She went into her site's design mode. As if she were on automatic pilot, she deleted Crushed's latest post and her whole exchange with him.

118

As if it never happened. Jen wouldn't need to know, right?

And Bonnie wouldn't have to read the stupid things she wrote ever again.

Bonnie logged off. The little hourglass flickered as the computer began to shut down. She crawled into bed. Finally the computer turned itself off leaving the room in darkness.

Exhausted, Bonnie still tossed and turned, unable to get comfortable. If only she could shut down her brain the way she shut down her computer, so that it was black and empty. But images and thoughts kept flickering in her head, making weird, unsettling patterns. Everything morphed and melted into each other—Jen and Tina crying, Julia crowing "pan-takes," Crushed's sad story, and then, Paolo touching her cheek....

Bonnie didn't think she fell asleep at all, but she must have drifted off because suddenly the birds were twittering outside and the sun was making golden stripes on the wall.

But it wasn't the birds that woke her up. Somehow, as she slept, a sudden thought had come crashing into her mind, with complete and utter certainty.

Crushed was none other than Carter.

And if that were true, it meant that the girl he had a crush on was *her*.

SURVIVAL SKILL #20:

A FRESH PERSPECTIVE CAN YIELD FRESH INSIGHTS.

Bonnie kept her head down at the breakfast table, staring bleakly into her untouched bowl of Cheerios. She knew she should eat it fast and get out of the kitchen on the double, before anyone else came down, but even so, the thought of lifting all those little o's to her mouth and actually swallowing them made her stomach heave. But she *had* to hurry. If Jen walked in, she'd take one look at Bonnie and know that Bonnie was keeping something from her. And boy, did she have something to hide.

Bonnie knew that if she told Jen about her Carter/Crushed revelation, she'd also have to reveal that she had blogged without her. So that meant Bonnie now had *two* secrets to keep.

But facing Jen still wasn't Bonnie's biggest worry. Having to go eyeball to eyeball with Carter over her cereal was even worse. The idea that he was thinking about her *in that way* made Bonnie's stomach almost turn inside out.

Luck was not on her side, though. Only moments later Carter bounded into the kitchen with Joe right on his heels. Jen followed a few seconds later, carrying Julia on her hip.

"Hey, guys," Carter said, yawning and rubbing his hair so it stood out in all directions. "I'm so fried. I stayed up too late. Cramming for exams."

The bile rose in Bonnie's throat.

Please don't look at me, Carter, she begged inside her head. *Please act like everything is normal.*

"That sucks," Joe said to Carter. "Bonnie, if you're not gonna eat that, can I have it?" He reached for her cereal bowl.

"Take it—I didn't even touch it."

"Ta. I need my strength today. Big game. So how was that party you guys went to on Friday? I don't think I've seen any of you all weekend."

"It was really fun," Jen said. "How was your date with whatsername… Mireille?"

Joe grimaced. "Don't even ask."

"Uh oh," Jen said. "So what happened?"

"What happened was I took her to the mall to go see a movie, and when we got there, she saw a bunch of her girlfriends out front. And they did that 'omigod, what are you doing here?' squeal-y thing you girls do, and were hugging each other like they hadn't just seen each other four hours before.

"Mireille's friends go, 'We were just heading over to Lick's to get something to eat.' And Mireille goes,

121

'C'mon Joe, let's go with them. They're like my *posse*—you can't say no.'

"So I say, 'OK, Mireille, but the movie's going to start pretty soon.'

"And she says, "We can go to a movie anytime, but when do I get to hang with my buds?"'

"Are you kidding?" Jen said. "That's so awful! I can't believe anyone would do that!"

"Tell me about it," Joe said with a sharp nod. "So I go, 'If I knew we were going to be hanging with your buds I would have brought my whole baseball team.' Then Mireille hands her cell phone over to me and says, 'Why don't you call them then, since you'd rather *be* with them?'

"So picture this: We're on our first 'date' and we're already having this argument in the mall with all these girls standing around us, hanging on every word, heads turning back and forth like they're watching a tennis match. I didn't exactly want to say, 'Mireille, I thought we'd be alone. That's kind of what a date is.' I thought that would make me sound like a suck. And by this point it seemed pretty clear Mireille really wasn't interested in me. If she were, she'd want to be with me, not hanging with her friends, right?"

"Bingo," Carter said.

"She sounds like a total you-know-what," Jen said.

"Yeah. So I said, 'I'm going to the Cineplex. Are you coming, Mireille? And I held her cell phone out to her.

"She takes it from me and says, cool as ice, 'That's

122

OK, Joe. Maybe next time?' So I turned around, walked away, and never looked back."

"Whoa, that's harsh," Carter said.

"I can't believe she would actually do that," Jen said. "I mean, you're such a nice guy."

"What I don't understand, is why she said yes when I asked her out, if she wasn't into me?" Joe said.

Carter glanced at Bonnie, then at Jen, and then quickly slid his eyes away from both of them. "Don't even try to understand 'em, bro. Girls are from another planet."

Bonnie's body went cold. Those words were hauntingly familiar.

"Hey—not all of us are like that," Jen said.

"Right—some of you are from a completely different galaxy." Joe punched Jen lightly in the arm.

"So I guess that triple date with the hunky brothers is out of the question, then, since I'm way out on Alpha Centauri?"

Carter spread his arms wide. "Who needs 'em? You've got the two hunkiest brothers in town right here—me and Joe. Am I right or am I right?"

"Definitely," nodded Joe, jokingly flexing first one bicep, then the other. "We've got the mojo. Whatever Mireille thinks."

"That's for sure," Jen said, smiling broadly.

Carter snapped his fingers and pointed at Jen. "So let's go out then—the four of us. This Saturday. I got passes for Canada's Wonderland. We can ride the 'coasters, do the bungie. My treat. Whaddya say?" He slapped Joe on the back.

Jen said, "Sure! That sounds like fun. I haven't been to Wonderland in years."

Joe said, "Count me in, too. No way am I going to sit at home and sulk." The three of them chattered excitedly, making plans. None of them seemed to notice that Bonnie didn't say a word.

She supposed they figured her silence meant "yes." What it really meant was this: *Please pretty please, oh please please please: let something happen that will get me off the hook. Something like double pneumonia or temporary blindness.* Because if they all went somewhere as a foursome, Bonnie knew exactly what would happen.

Jen would stick to Joe like glue. By default, then, Bonnie would wind up riding the roller coasters with Carter, a.k.a. Crushed. Who would thus have a perfectly good excuse for putting his arm around her and making a move.

"I think I'm gonna be sick," Bonnie said and bolted from the room.

SURVIVAL SKILL #21:

TAKE THE BULL BY THE HORNS.

That afternoon, Tina came over. She grabbed a cup of coffee and went into Bonnie's bedroom to visit with her girls.

Bonnie's mother had said that half of Tina's problem was that she just needed a good night's sleep. Bonnie figured her mom was right because after only one night on her own, Tina looked like a million bucks. With her hair loose around her shoulders, sitting cross-legged on Bonnie's bed, she could easily pass for Jen's big sister.

Bonnie did a quick calculation in her head. Tina was thirty-two. That meant she was only seventeen when she'd gotten pregnant with Jen, maybe eighteen when Jen was born. That was even younger than Celia was now. Bonnie had to give her head a shake. She couldn't even imagine what that must have been like.

Tina was telling Jen that she'd talked with her supervisor and had made her promise that she wouldn't put Tina on nights for at least a month. That way, she could get some solid sleep, and have the afternoons and evenings free to spend with Jen and Julia. She also said she'd found out where AA meetings were held in the area.

"I'm going to start going again, Jen. I'll get a sponsor and I swear I will do everything I can *not* to touch a drink again. E-V-E-R." She spelled out the word.

"That's really good, Tina," Jen said. Bonnie could tell Jen really wanted to believe her, but that she was still being cautious. Tina always meant what she said. It was following through that was her problem.

"So how was your day, Bonnie?" Tina asked. "Anything exciting going on in your world?"

Jen jumped in, her voice a teasing sing-song. "Bonnie met a *guyyyyy*. On the weekend..."

"Yeah," Bonnie said, suddenly feeling oddly shy.

"Do tell," Tina said enthusiastically. "I want to hear all about him!"

Now, Bonnie had been holding the memory of Paolo close, like he was her own special secret, throughout every minute of every one of the previous, tumultuous days. With everything else that had been going on, though, there had been hardly any opportunity for her to talk to anyone about what had happened. She'd barely even been able to think about it.

But now that Tina had asked, it was like the dam had broken. And out it all spilled—the blow-by-blow of the party, of dancing, of talking for hours. Bonnie felt as if she could go on and on—just saying his name out loud was a thrill.

"So has he called you yet?" Tina asked, her eyes bright with excitement.

"Not yet, but it's exam week. Paolo's got to study. He said he'll call toward the end of the week. He said maybe we'd do something on the weekend."

"He's incredibly cute," Jen said. "Like a Calvin Klein model."

Tina wagged her finger at Bonnie. "You got to watch out for guys that look like that. Heartbreakers."

"Don't say that!" Jen scolded. "He hasn't done anything except be gorgeous and have excellent taste in girls. Give him a chance. All guys aren't rotters, you know."

Tina sighed. "I know. There are some good ones out there. OK, so forget I said anything. He's gorgeous, and he's nice, and he's going to call, like, any minute. *Mazel tov*. So what about you, Jen? Did you meet someone at the party, too?"

Jen flicked her hair out of her face. "Not exactly. But there is someone I have my eye on…."

Tina raised one eyebrow. "And…?"

"And nothing. Not yet anyway. But I'm working on it."

"That's my girl!" Tina said, giving Jen a pinch on the cheek. "Watch out world!"

Or rather, Bonnie thought, *watch out, Joe! Jen has got her sights set on you…and Carter has his sights set on me*.

Bonnie shuddered.

In that instant, Bonnie made up her mind. There was *no way* she was going to go to Wonderland with Carter as her "date." All that she needed was the perfect excuse to get out of it.

Bonnie was pondering the mechanics of faking a twenty-four hour flu when the solution hit her. She couldn't believe she hadn't thought of it before.

Why should she get stuck with Carter? Didn't she already have a guy in her life? A fabulous Beautiful Boy of her very own?

Even better, she'd been dying to talk to Paolo for sixty-three solid hours. Now she had a reason to pick up the phone and call *him*. Of course he'd want to go— exams would be over by then. And what was better than being a teenager in Wonderland on a warm spring night?

Bonnie imagined strolling through Wonderland with Paolo at her side. It gave her shivers just thinking about it. She pictured holding hands with him on the spinning swings…sharing an ice cream cone…cuddling up with him on the swan boats…kissing in the dark…

Then Bonnie realized that although Paolo had taken her cell number, she had never thought to ask for his.

But before she could dissolve in a hissy fit of frustration, a deliciously evil idea crossed her mind.

Why not kill two birds with one stone?

SURVIVAL SKILL #22:

MEDITATE.

Bonnie knocked on Carter's door.

"*Entrez,*" he said.

"Sorry to bug you," Bonnie said, "but—"

"No probs! Come in! Come in!" Carter swept some text books and papers off of a chair and waved her into it. "Welcome to my pad. *Mi casa es su casa.*"

Bonnie looked around—she didn't think she'd actually ever been in his room. The last time she'd stepped over that threshold was before he'd moved in, when the room had still been Celia's.

Instead of Flower Power and Day-glo, Carter had a Zen thing going on. He had a futon bed on a low platform, a long, low coffee table as a nightstand, and a lot of squooshy pillows in warm shades of rust and red. They made the room feel welcoming and serene. A tray on the nightstand held one rock, a single pine cone, and a flickering red candle. The room smelled good, too—like green tea.

"Wow," Bonnie said, her eyebrows rising up almost to her hairline. "It's nice in here. Who decorated it for you?"

"Nobody. I did it myself. A can of paint and a couple of knick-nacks go a long way."

"It's great! Really," Bonnie replied, even more surprised than before.

"Thanks. It was no big deal. It's humble, like me. But hey, it's home." He gave Bonnie his big, toothy 'Carter the Stud' grin. She pointed to a delicate Japanese scroll hanging over the desk. "That's neat. Where did you get that?"

"The scroll? It's called a *kakejiku*. I made it," said Carter.

Bonnie couldn't believe her ears. "You MADE it? You're kidding! It's gorgeous! Who taught you how to do that calligraphy?"

Carter shrugged. "I found a picture of it in an art book I picked up at a second-hand shop. It appealed to me. I just copied it, is all. No big."

Bonnie blinked, and blinked again. Her logic circuits sputtered. Had she heard Carter correctly?

Bonnie felt more than a little disoriented. She heard herself gush, "That is so amazing! I had no idea you were artistic like that. Does the writing mean anything?"

"Yes. It says, 'Life is suffering'."

"Life is *suffering*?" she raised her eyebrows again at him. Who *was* this guy? Not the Carter she knew. It felt like the pod people had come and swapped Pinky with The Brain.

"It's not really like it sounds, Bonnie. 'Life is suffering' is actually the First Sacred Truth of Buddhism. And it doesn't really mean that life sucks or anything. What it means is that if you get too caught up in the everyday stuff, you're bound to suffer. You've got to learn to detach. Knowing how to detach is key to surviving. For me, anyway. I've learned you just got to let things chill, you know?"

"Since when did you become a Buddhist?" Bonnie asked, thoroughly floored.

"I'm not. Not yet, anyway. But that doesn't mean you can't learn something from them. Or that what other cultures have to say can't be useful."

Bonnie was more than a little shocked. She had never heard him sounding so thoughtful before. Serious ideas never came out of his mouth. Not when he was around her, anyway.

"Sure," Bonnie said vaguely and then gave her head a shake. It was time to get to the reason for her 'visit' before she totally lost her own focus.

"Um, Carter, I just wanted to ask you. Do you have Paolo Rossi's phone number? He gave it to me at the dance but I must have deleted it by accident." She could feel the tips of her ears start to burn red.

"Paolo? Really? Why—oh, yeah! I remember! I saw you dancing with him at the Bash."

He looked Bonnie up and down. "Sooooo you're into him, then? I never would have guessed our man the *Conquistadore* was your type. Yep, you are full of surprises, Lady Bon, full o' surprises." His voice held both admiration and a smirk.

Clearly, Bonnie thought, *real Carter was still inside the pod. It was only the shell that had gotten a buff.* "The phone number...?" she said coldly.

131

"Right. Yeah, I got it. Hold on a sec." Carter leaned across the nightstand to his desk drawer and pulled out a sheaf of papers. It was a school directory.

"It'll be in here," he said.

While he flipped through the pages, Bonnie thought about the nickname he'd called Paolo, the *konkeesta*-something. Even though she was trying to seem cool and "detached," it had piqued her interest.

"Um, Carter…What was that nickname you called him? I hadn't heard anyone use it before…"

He stopped flipping pages and his eyes met hers. "*Il Conquistadore?* It's just something the guys came up with. It's Italian. For 'The Conqueror.' Paolo has a way with the ladies, you know?"

He studied Bonnie through half-lidded eyes. "So, are you and Paolo like a 'thang?'" He made quotation marks with his fingers in the air.

Bonnie felt a sudden flame of anger. Where did Carter get off talking to her like that? He made her feel like the time she'd spent with Paolo was sordid and cheap. Like it meant nothing. Like *she* meant nothing.

Hold on, Bonnie, she thought, taking a deep breath. *Just get the number and get out of here. Don't lose it on him—put on your plastic smile and pretend you don't hate his guts.* Bonnie took the rock from the nightstand and hefted it in her hand. It felt smooth, solid. *Steadying.* "Not exactly," she said, smiling her fake smile, "but we said we'd get together again on the weekend. I want to touch base with him before we make all those

Wonderland plans." *Now just give me the number and let me outta here.*

"Cool," he said, nodding as he put his thumb in a page of the directory. "Hnhh. His cell's not listed in here. But here's the number of the res' hall phone—you can reach him on that. You got a pen?"

Bonnie grabbed a sticky note and a pen off of his desk. She took the directory from Carter and copied out the number.

While she wrote, Carter leaned back against an oversized bolster. "You know," he mused, "that guy sure can party…You should have seen him in action at the Christmas Do. Or maybe it was the Valentine's Dance…"

Then he sat up straight. "Hey! Bonbon!—I've got a brainstorm happening. Why don't you ask him to come to Wonderland with us? Maybe we can put something big together, get lots of people out— a total party scene. That would be so awesome!"

Bonnie paused with her hand in mid-air as she was about to slip the paper in her pocket. If Carter were Crushed, he wouldn't be inviting Paolo to Wonderland with them, would he?

But if he wasn't, how could she have been *so sure* that he *was* Crushed?

And if she had been wrong about Carter, how many other things was she wrong about?

SURVIVAL SKILL #23:

PATIENCE IS A VIRTUE.

Back in the safety of her room, Bonnie shook herself out of her fog. She figured it must have been the smell of the candle that had made her feel so off balance. At least, that's what she told herself.

So maybe Carter wasn't Crushed after all. *Whatever,* she thought. She'd worry about Carter later. But now she had to find the nerve to call Paolo and figure out what to say once she got him on the phone.

She practiced different approaches in her head.

"Hey! How's it going? Just wanted to find out if you're free on Saturday...

"Hi! I was thinking about you and wondering if you wanted to go to Wonderland with me on Saturday.

"Listen, a bunch of us are going to Wonderland on Saturday and I was thinking you might want to bring along some of the guys..."

Each sounded lamer than the last. Finally, Bonnie decided to wing it. She'd just wait 'til he was on the other end of the phone, and take it from there.

Bonnie listened for a moment. She heard Tina and

134

Jennifer saying goodbye to each other at the door and Julia cooing sweetly between them. That was good—she could have total privacy when she made the call, without having to resort to phoning from the bathroom.

She closed her door and made sure it was locked. Her heart was beating so hard she could feel it in her ears. Her hands were all cold and clammy. Her fingers kept slipping as she tried to dial. She messed up about four times and kept having to start over.

Finally, Bonnie pressed talk and listened to the little bleeps as the connection went through. At the other end, the phone in the dorm started to ring.

It rang.

And rang.

And rang.

Bonnie thought, *Great, no one will pick up. All of this anxiety for nothing.*

She was just about to hang up and try to figure out a Plan B when someone answered the phone.

"Yo! Benny's Pizza House."

"Hi! Is this the residence hall?" she managed with a squeak.

"Yeah. Who d'ya want?"

"May I speak with Paolo Rossi, please?"

"Hang on." She could hear the phone clatter as the boy left it dangling. In the distance, she heard him shouting, "Yo! Rossi! Hall phone for you."

There was some more clattering, then some laughter, and a conversation in the background Bonnie couldn't really make out. Then she heard the boy saying, "Another chick…I dunno, I didn't ask. Why don't you get it yourself from now on, man? I'm not your message boy."

Bonnie waited nervously. The phone clattered again. Someone was picking it up.

"He can't come to the phone now. Can he call you back?" said the same boy who had answered in the first place.

Bonnie's heart sank.

"Um, yeah," she said, biting her lip. "Can you tell him it's Bonnie? And I'll be home all night?"

"Yeah sure."

"Thanks," Bonnie said. She was about to offer her phone number again, but the boy had already hung up.

Bonnie swore silently to herself. She had managed to work up her confidence to make the call, and then, nothing. She was back where she started, waiting for Paolo to call her.

She stuck her cell in her pocket. She wasn't going to go *anywhere* without it—not even to the washroom.

Bonnie heard her doorknob rattle. "Bonnie?" Jen called through the locked door.

"Just a minute," Bonnie said, running to let her in.

"What's up? You never lock your door."

Bonnie told her about her call to Paolo.

"Wow—you're brave. I'd never have the nerve to call a boy like that."

"I don't know. I think waiting for the guys to call us is even worse. I hate being out of control of the situation

136

like that. Plus I hate suspense. And worrying that maybe he won't call."

"Why wouldn't he call? You said you had an amazing time together."

Bonnie nodded. "Yeah, we did." She smiled, remembering.

"So when's he calling you back? Later?"

"I guess so. The guy who answered the phone didn't say."

"Then let's go for our run now. You'll be all relaxed for his call after you work out."

So Jen and Bonnie went for a nice long 10K run.

Bonnie's phone didn't ring once the whole time.

They ate dinner. They did their homework. They checked their blog. There was a new question.

 Dear Bonnie and Jen,

My three best friends have all decided to get tattoos. They want me to get the same one as them so that we are like our own special 'sisterhood' thing.
I love my gals, I really do, but I do NOT want to get a tattoo. Plus my mom and dad would absolutely MURDERIZE me if they found out I'd gotten a picture of Hello Kitty on my butt.
How can I tell my friends 'I'm out' without them kicking me out of our friendship?"
—Butt No

○ Dear Butt No,

Cool! I've always wanted a tattoo! But yeah, my parents would murderize me, too. And if I was going to get murderized for permanently inking my butt, I'd want to make sure I was doing it for the right reason. Like because I wanted to do it, not because someone else was telling me I HAD to do it. Tell your kitty-cat gals exactly what you told us—that you love them from the bottom of your butt, but your butt is a "butt-out" zone, and tattoos are not your style. If they are your real friends, they'll understand your feelings and the case will be closed.

 • I agree with Bonnie, but I realize that friendships aren't always as neat and perfect as we would like, and feelings aren't either. The way you describe it, it sounds like your friends have put a lot on this tattoo idea—for them, maybe, it symbolizes something more than just a lark. It could mean swearing loyalty to each other. A kind of 'all for one, one for all' thing. Your question might really be deeper than just how to tell them, "Thanks, but no thanks."

Perhaps what you're really wondering is if this group is for you, and/or if they are going in directions you don't want to travel. And if you say no on this issue, what will that mean in the future? Will they continue on together, a merry threesome, without you? And where will that leave you? Are you ready to stand on your own, as an independent person, or do you really feel like you need to be part of this clique to survive?

 ○ Because as we are here to tell you, you will survive, with or without them. What's most important is, can you live with yourself and your own decisions? If you went ahead and got the tattoo, even if your folks never found out, how will you feel in ten years—or even next month—when you see it in the mirror? And what if your friendship fizzles? Then you'd be stuck with the stupid tattoo—a painful memory of a friendship that's history.

 • Exactly.
Pardon the pun, but in the end, you can only do what's right for you. Tell them how you feel. If you're lucky, they'll be like, "OK, no problem." If they turn jerkish on you, well, better to find that out now rather than after you are marked for life.

So we say, good luck, keep your nose—and tush—clean, and remember,

You will survive!!!!!
Love, Bonnie and Jen

SURVIVAL SKILL #24:

PATIENCE IS A VIRTUE PART 2.

There was still no call from Paolo. Bonnie checked her phone again and again, hoping she hadn't missed his call by accident. Or that she *had* missed his call by accident. But either way, it didn't matter. There was nothing in her voice mailbox. Just that computery voice, saying, "You have NO new messages."

Bonnie took her shower. She dried her hair. She read a magazine.

Still no call.

She gave her mom a kiss goodnight. She kissed Julia, asleep in her crib. She shouted out a goodnight to Otto.

No call.

She changed from her robe to her pajamas.

She said goodnight to Jen and turned out the lights.

Still no call.

Lying in the dark, Bonnie fretted. *Why hadn't Paolo called back?*

Maybe he'd gotten bogged down in studying. Or worse—maybe he'd lost her phone number?

This really sucks! Bonnie thought. She wanted to

scream. She hated being in limbo, and now she was in even worse limbo than before.

There was no way she could sleep. She looked over at Jen, who had crashed out pretty hard.

Bonnie realized she had never told her about the weird conversation she'd had with Carter. She knew Jen would have found it funny—him doing Japanese calligraphy (!) and talking about Buddhist Sacred Truths (!). That wasn't the Carter they both knew and loathed….

Bonnie went over their conversation in her mind again.

"Why don't you ask him to come to Wonderland with us?" Carter had said.

That definitely didn't sound like a guy with a crush, not one on *her* anyway. So maybe Carter wasn't Crushed after all….

But if he wasn't Crushed, then who was?

The temptation to find out gnawed at her. *Should she try to find out?* No, she scolded herself. That wouldn't be right. One of the principles of the Survive blog was that it was anonymous.

But still…wasn't this a unique case? One to which the normal rules didn't apply?

Perhaps, she told herself, it would be OK to just go online and see if Crushed was all right. And if, by the by, she found out a little bit more about him—like who he might or might not be—well, that wouldn't be breaking the rules, would it?

Bonnie silently made her way to the computer and

turned it on. She wrung her hands as she waited for their homepage to come up.

Nothing. No message from Crushed. No message from Invisible. No message from anyone.

Bonnie put her fingers on the keys.

"Crushed?" she wrote. "Are you there?"

There was no answer.

Disappointed, Bonnie put the computer to sleep and crawled back into bed. Despite her nervous state, fatigue washed over her. She felt it pulling her down, deeper and deeper. She let it drag her along, and with relief, she gave herself over to sleep.

The next thing Bonnie knew, it was morning. Julia was bouncing on her bed, pulling on her blankets and shouting in her ear, "Wake up, Bonn-eeeee! Pan-takes are red-eeeee!"

It had been eighty long hours since Bonnie had spoken to Paolo.

Eighty hours and still counting.

SURVIVAL SKILL #25:

BE PREPARED TO BITE THE BULLET.

It was Thursday. Paolo still hadn't called. Bonnie was definitely getting a bad feeling. *If he felt anything like the way she did, how come he wasn't calling, like, a hundred times a day?*

Bonnie reluctantly forced herself to consider what she'd overheard while waiting for Paolo to come to the phone. In the background, the boy who had answered her call, saying, "Another chick...I dunno, I didn't ask."

Did that mean Paolo was getting calls from lots of girls? Was he using this other kid to screen his calls? And if so, did it mean that he had decided not to call back?

Bonnie shoved the idea to the back of her mind. Now that would be crazy. After all, they'd had such a great time together—she wasn't imagining *that*.

That afternoon, as usual, Jen and Bonnie walked home from school together. Jen knew right away what was on Bonnie's mind.

"Just call him again," she said. "If he lost your number, he'll never be able to call you."

"But maybe he doesn't want to call me," Bonnie said, clutching her stomach. It felt like she had swallowed a fistful of rocks.

"Then find out once and for all! Don't put yourself through this. Make the call; talk to him. If he's not interested, you'll find out. It will suck, but then it will be over and you can move on."

"I don't want it to be over," Bonnie said. And then she started to cry—big, hot tears that wouldn't stop.

"No, I guess not," Jen said, putting her arm around her. "But if he's not interested, it already *is* over."

"Gee, thanks."

"All I mean is that you should just find out where you stand. It probably is nothing, right? He lost your number, or couldn't call for some really good but stupid reason.

"Why don't you call him right now? I'll sit right here with you." She pointed to a bench. "If things are good, I'll buy you a pop to celebrate. If things go south, I'll buy you a pop to drown your sorrows, OK?"

Bonnie wiped her eyes and nodded.

"I don't want him to know I was crying though. I have to sound strong, confident."

Jen sang out, "You've got so much love to give, so much life to live, you will survive…!"

Bonnie started to laugh and joined in with her on the chorus: "I will survive, I will survive!"

Jen pressed the phone into Bonnie's hand. "Call.

144

While you're still feeling girl power."

Bonnie went into her phonebook and selected the dorm phone number. She pressed TALK.

The phone line rang.

And rang.

She rolled her eyes at Jen and held up a finger for each ring. She was at eight fingers when the phone was picked up, at last, at the other end.

"*Pronto?*"

'Hello' in Italian.

"Um…Is this Paolo?" Bonnie asked, trying to keep the nerves out of her voice.

"Yes…"

"Hi, Paolo. It's me! Bonnie."

"Oh—hello, Bonnie! From the dance! So, how are you?"

"I'm good…And you?"

"Fine, fine," he said. "You know, the usual."

"Listen," Bonnie said, after an awkward pause, "I wanted, um, to ask you something. A bunch of us, we're, um…like, if you could, um, like, go to Canada's Wonderland with a bunch of us. We're thinking of going Saturday night…"

"Is that the amusement park?" Paolo asked. "I have never been there. It sounds like fun…but I'm so sorry, I can't go. I have something to do…my uncle, he is in town for the weekend from Torino…."

"Oh," Bonnie squeaked. "The whole weekend?"

"Yes, he is visiting until Tuesday."

There was a long silence while Bonnie waited for Paolo

to say, "But I still want to see you sometime soon…"

"Paolo? I had been, um…I mean, I'd been kinda hoping to hear from you," she said.

"Oh….Oh, man. It's really hard right now. It is exam time, you know? I'm really busy now."

She waited, again, for him to say something else. He didn't. The silence was horrible. She could hear his faint breathing on the other end of the line. She could imagine him doodling on the wall, drawing a heart with a big black X over it.

"I see," Bonnie said at last.

Jen sighed and put a comforting hand on her shoulder.

"I just thought that…I was looking forward to…you know," Bonnie rambled on, stumbling over her words. She knew she should just shut up and try and collect what little was left of her dignity, but she couldn't.

"Hold on a second—just one second, Bonnie." Paolo put his hand over the mouthpiece. Bonnie could hear shuffling and scraping sounds, then a short laugh. Paolo came back on the line. "Another guy here needs the phone. I have to go. It was nice to talk to you. I'll call you, OK? Soon!"

"Yeah, sure," Bonnie said.

"Okay then! *Ciao!*"

"Bye then." Her voice had become a whisper.

He hung up.

Bonnie pressed END.

She looked up at Jen. "He said he'd call me," she managed through her tears. "Soon."

146

"Oh, Bonnie, I'm so sorry…" Jen said, hugging her.

"But maybe he really will. Maybe next week, don't you think?" Bonnie said hopefully, the tears running freely down her cheeks.

"Sure he will," Jennifer said. But Bonnie knew as well as Jen did what "I'll call you" meant. If it wasn't followed by "tomorrow after school," or "and we can make plans for which movie we want to go to on Saturday," it was as good as saying, *Arrivaderci,* have a nice life.

Bonnie's love life had barely even begun. And surprise, surprise—it was already over.

Dear Bonnie,

You were right.

I didn't like what you wrote but I have to admit that there is something to what you say about wanting to cause a little "kaboom!" of my own. Is that really why I keep obsessing about her? Who knows. And I guess in the end it doesn't really matter. What does matter is if I came on to her, the you-know-what would definitely hit the fan. Can you imagine the aggro? "He's hitting on his own sister—what a total creep!"

It's not what's in your head that counts, it's what you *do.* So I'm gonna take your advice and keep my yap shut. And maybe I'll take up a new hobby, like whittling or throat-singing or bridge. That should keep me out of the house and away from her.

What I really need is to meet someone else. Someone like you.

But you're probably in Flin Flon or Gander or Back-o-beyond or something. And here I am in the Big Smoke—typing in the middle of the night. What a dink, eh?

Talk to you soon?

—Crushed and Flattened

SURVIVAL SKILL #26:

KNOW WHO YOUR TRUE FRIENDS ARE.

Jen handed Bonnie another tissue.

"But it doesn't make any sense!" Bonnie cried.

"Who said boys make sense, Bon? Have you ever known a boy to actually make *sense?*" Jen asked.

"But I thought Paolo was different!" Bonnie blew her nose and dropped the tissue into the overflowing wastebasket at her side.

"Yeah, so he said some pretty words and danced great and made you feel special. Guys do that from time to time."

"Why bother to *pretend* to like someone?" Bonnie said, getting more and more agitated. "Why tell them all those things to get their minds going, and then go, 'Ha ha! The joke's on you!'? I JUST DON'T GET IT!" She picked up a stuffed Sponge Bob that was sitting on her nightstand and hurled it at the wall.

"Whoa, flying sea creatures! Everybody duck!" Joe had stuck his head into Bonnie's room just as Sponge Bob sailed across the room. "Is everything OK in here?"

Jen crossed her arms and gave Joe an exasperated look. "Maybe you can explain why guys do stuff that

149

doesn't make sense. I'm not making any headway, here."

"Easy," Joe said, scooping up Bob and sitting him on top of his head. "We're jerks."

"Cut it out," Bonnie said. "You are not going to make me laugh."

Joe exchanged a glance with Jen. "Ooooh—that sounds like a challenge!"

He did a silly clown walk and then pretended to present Jen with flowers, giving her Sponge Bob instead. She curtsied and took the toy, then pitched it right at Bonnie. Then she jumped on her. "Tickle torture!"

Joe got right in there. He stuck his fingers in her armpit and wiggled them, while Jen held her down and gave her a raspberry on her ankle. Bonnie was howling at them to stop, laughing and crying at the same time.

"Leave me alone! Can't you see I'm not laughing?"

"Looks like you're laughing to me," Carter said "Is this an invitation-only party or can anyone join in?"

"All of you—get out of here! NOW!" Bonnie yelled. She guessed she must have sounded really mad because both Jen and Joe let go of her at the same time and stepped away.

"Look, Bonnie," Jen said, "I know you're upset. But the guy's a jerk. So don't give him the satisfaction of ruining your day, OK? You had a good time with him at a party. Fine. So you would have liked there to be more. But it could be worse. You could have spent the night dancing with *him*." Jen stuck out her thumb and pointed it at Carter.

150

"Yeah." Carter nodded. "Wait—what?"

"Or watching your brother getting his manhood cut to ribbons by Mireille the Monster," Joe said.

"I'm guessing *Il Conquistatore* did his patented cut and run?" asked Carter.

"Oh, it's *patented* now? Does everybody know something here except me?" Bonnie wailed.

"The guy's nickname is the Conquerer, *chica* . That's a pretty good clue he has some experience in the love 'em and leave 'em department," Jen said.

"I *did* try to tell you," Carter said.

"What do you mean you tried to tell me? Tell me what?" Bonnie said angrily. "Did you know this guy was a turd? Coz you didn't say a word…."

"I did. I told you he had a rep, Bonnie. 'A way with the ladies,' I said. But let's be honest here—even if I had told you flat out, 'Stay away from him, he's trouble,' would you have listened to me? I don't think so. Since when do you listen to anything 'Carter the Crinoid' has to say? Don't look so innocent and shocked, Bonnie. I know you call me that, you and Jen, when you think I'm not around."

Bonnie blushed furiously. "Why don't you just get lost, Carter, and get out of my life! You can take your stupid kamikaze scroll and your Seven Sacred whatevers and your stupid Upper Crust College pals and shove them right up your Manse. Then you won't have to worry about my little problems any more, OK?" She was overflowing with rage—at Paolo, at Carter, at the whole stupid world. She wished everyone would just drop dead, right then and there. *Especially* Carter.

"Hold on, hold on," Joe said, coming between Carter and Bonnie. "He was only trying to help. And Carter, don't listen to her. You know she shoots her mouth off like a Roman Candle every chance she gets. So just everybody chill, OK?

"The truth is this guy Paolo hosed you, Bonnie. He gave you a line and you fell for it. Why not? He was good-looking—not as good-looking as me, I daresay, but good-looking all the same. He danced you off your feet and whispered sweet nothings in your ear.

"So you bit. Maybe it was the first time for you, but guaranteed, it won't be the last."

"How could I be such a sucker?" Bonnie said, knuckling her eyes. "I am SO stupid."

Then Carter broke in. "Listen up. I'm not supposed to tell you this. But you know my man, Dan? He was pretty upset when he saw you waltz off with Rossi. He had a pretty good idea this might happen—he used to room with the guy. He knows Rossi's *modus operandi,* shall we say. Slick as a—"

"Dan? Your friend Dan talked about me and Paolo to you?" Bonnie gaped. "The same Dan who ignored me all night? Why on earth would *he* care? He didn't say two words to me the whole time I was with him. He treated me like I was dog poop on his shoe!"

Carter grabbed Bonnie's desk chair. He pulled it around and straddled it backward, with his arms on the backrest.

"Maybe if you weren't so quick to judge, Miss Sweeta Bonita, you would have noticed that Dan was

152

not ignoring you. Truth is, he was *scared* of you. He didn't talk to you because he was so flipping nervous. He's a pretty shy guy and he thought you were—lemme see, how did he describe you? 'She makes Megan Fox look like a skank.' He finally worked up his courage to talk to you and whammo! You were gone with the *Conquistatore*."

"Now that's good news," Jen said brightly. "Someone likes you, other than Joe and me."

Bonnie put her head in her hands. "I don't believe this. I am soooo confused!"

"See?" Joe said. "We guys *are* jerks. Just ignore everything we say. You can only trust us when we're not talking."

"So shut up, then," Jen said.

"*Dan* likes me?" Bonnie said again, trying to get her head around it.

"Yeah. He likes you," Carter said. "I don't know why, the way you ditched him at the dance like that. Left him searching for you like a lost puppy." He held up his hands like he was reading a sign on a lamp post. 'LOST: Purebred Beauty. Answers to the name of 'Yowza!' Last seen: sniffing a slimedog's butt.' And he's been worrying about you ever since."

Everything just seemed to get curiouser and curiouser.

"Worrying? About *me*? Why?" Bonnie squeaked.

"He was fretting all week that you were going to get the Paolo Heave-Ho. He didn't think it was going to be pretty. Call him crazy, but he didn't want you to get hurt."

153

"So what's with this Paolo guy, anyway?" Jen grilled Carter. "Is he seriously psycho or just meaner than dirt? Does he think he gets points for every girl he twists into a knot? And 50,000 points gets him free admission to Euro Disney?"

"Who knows?" Carter said, shrugging his shoulders. "I don't waste my time thinking about him. All I know is that for some reason, girls love him. Meanwhile every guy wants to pound him one."

"Hey," Joe said. "Have I got the perfect girl for him!"

"Let me guess," Bonnie said. "Mireille?"

"Wouldn't that be A1? They could dump each other simultaneously. See who bounces higher."

Bonnie looked from Jen, to Joe, to Carter and back again. They were being so good to her—true friends. She reached out her hands to Jen and to Joe.

"Thanks, guys. All of you," she said. "I mean it. I don't know what I'd do without you."

Carter pointed to himself, then pretended to look over his first his left shoulder and then his right.

"Yeah, even you, Carter. You crinoid," Bonnie said, picking up the Sponge Bob and thwacking him in the arm with it.

"Hey—be nice to the Bobster. He's a good guy," Carter said, grabbing Sponge Bob out of her hand. He let the toy dangle from his fingers by one skinny leg. "Um, since we're having such a rare family moment—and for the record—what the heck is a crinoid anyway?"

Jen caught Bonnie's eye. She looked from Bonnie,

to Carter with Sponge Bob on his finger, and back to Bonnie again. It was just too perfect. The girls started to giggle.

Once they started, they couldn't stop. Before long, Jen was rolling on the bed beside Bonnie, clutching her sides and howling with laughter. Bonnie was laughing so hard she thought she would pee her pants. It just felt so good to be laughing after all the tension.

"What? What's so funny?" asked Carter. He was annoyed, but the laughter was catching. He couldn't help smiling and even started to laugh a bit himself. "Come on—tell me."

Bonnie backhanded Sponge Bob, making him swing back and forth. "A crinoid," she spluttered, between hoots and snorts of laughter, "is a primitive…sea…creature!!!! You…and 'the Bobster'…are a perfect pair!"

Life sucks. Life sucks. Life sucks. Life
sucks. Life sucks. Life sucks. Life sucks.
Life sucks. Life sucks. Life sucks. Life
sucks. Life sucks. Life sucks. Life sucks.
Life sucks. Life sucks. Life sucks.
Life sucks. Life sucks. Life sucks. Life
sucks. Life sucks. Life sucks. Life sucks.
Life sucks. **Life sucks.** Life sucks. Life
sucks. Life sucks. Life sucks. Life sucks.
Life sucks. Life sucks. Life sucks. Life sucks.
Life sucks. Life sucks. Life sucks.
Life sucks. Life sucks. Life sucks. Life
sucks. Life sucks. Life sucks. Life sucks.
Life sucks. Life sucks. Life sucks. Life
sucks. Life sucks. Life sucks. Life sucks.
Life sucks. Life sucks. Life sucks. Life
sucks. Life sucks. Life sucks. Life sucks.
Life sucks. Life sucks. Life sucks. Life
sucks. Life sucks. Life sucks. Life sucks. Life
sucks. Life sucks. Life sucks. Life sucks.
Life sucks. Life sucks. Life sucks. Life
sucks. Life sucks. Life sucks. Life sucks.
Life sucks. Life sucks. Life sucks. Life
sucks. Life sucks. Life sucks. Life sucks.
Life sucks. **Life sucks.** Life sucks. Life
sucks. Life sucks. Life sucks. Life sucks.
Life sucks. Life sucks. Life **sucks.** Life
sucks. Life sucks. Life sucks. Life sucks.
Life sucks. Life sucks. Life sucks.

SURVIVAL SKILL #27:

TRUST YOUR INSTINCTS.

O f course, Bonnie couldn't sleep. She was still plagued with leftover doubts and insecurities that even the new revelations about Dan couldn't totally wash away.

She glanced to her left and could see that Jen was having trouble sleeping, too. She kept making these huge sighs and rolling over in bed. Bonnie knew why—Tina had called earlier that day and said she wanted Jen and Julia to come back home after the weekend. Jen was not sure if she should go or not. She was still kind of mad at Tina, and still not certain that Tina was really ready yet.

Bonnie and Jen talked the whole thing over with Bonnie's mom before going to bed. On the pro side, Jen knew that Tina had done everything she had promised. She had talked to her boss and told her about her problem. She was now going to get some help and support services through the hospital she worked at.

Tina had also found two different AA groups and had started going to both—one during the week and one on weekends. She had gotten a sponsor who would help her through rough times so Tina wouldn't backslide and take another drink. She'd also gone to see her family doctor and was making plans for the family to go to a therapist. So even though it was 99.99999% decided that Jen and Julia would go back home on Sunday, Bonnie knew Jen wasn't feeling totally easy in her mind.

"If I don't go home," Jen had said, "that'd be sending a message that I don't trust her, or that I'm, like, rejecting her. And I don't want to do that. After all, if she does all the right things, shouldn't I be there for her? But still, I know I'm going to feel like I'm walking on eggshells all the time. I'm still so bleeping mad."

Now, as Bonnie peered through the darkness, she could tell that Jen was still wide awake. "Are you OK?"

"You're up, too?"

"Yeah," Bonnie said. "I feel too miserable to sleep. I wish I could. Then I would forget that I'd just had my heart ripped out of my body and stepped on by a herd of wild buffalo."

Jen sat up and rubbed her eyes. "I think I'm going downstairs to heat up some warm milk. That always helps me calm down. It might make us sleepy enough to drop off. Do you want me to bring you a mug?"

"No, thanks. I hate the stuff. But go ahead. I'm going to check the blog."

"OK…I doubt there'll be anything, though. You said there hasn't been anything all week." Jen pulled on her robe and padded off to the kitchen.

Bonnie wrapped her quilt around her shoulders and booted up the computer. There was another message from Crushed.

Dear Bonnie,

I didn't hear back from you after my last post. I hope everything's OK. I miss "talking" to you.

—Crushed

○ Hi. I guess you could say everything's OK. If getting kicked in the teeth and having your heart stepped on is OK.

I'm having a pretty rotten time today. To make a long story short, I thought there was somebody special in my life. And it turned out he was just a lying, deceiving creepazoid. So I'm just sitting here feeling sorry for myself. Wondering if perhaps you are there too?

Bonnie checked the clock—it was about the same time of night as her last virtual conversation with Crushed. She hit enter and waited to see if Crushed would reply.

Her heart skipped a beat when a post appeared.

➢"Hi. Yeah, I'm here. Nothing better to do but stare at a blank screen. But it's not blank anymore. You're there! I'm really glad. It sounds like you got dumped. Ouch.

 ○ How does my step-brother from another planet put it? "Like I got thrown from a plane at 3000 feet." He didn't even wait for the splat.

 ➢That's rough. Sorry to hear it. Would it help if I told you the guy's probably not worth your while anyway?

 ○ I don't think so. Maybe in a year or two, but now it would be like putting a band aid on a bullet wound.

 ➢I hear you. So let's distract you from the wound. What else is happening? Where is Jen? She's not posting anymore.

 ○ She's got her own garbage to get through.

 ➢That's too bad. So maybe the pair of you are not in such good shape for giving advice to those of us in cyberspace. Sounds like you can use some.

○ It had crossed my mind.

 ≫ So here's my advice for you: meet a new guy.

 ○ Gee, thanks, C! *smacking forehead* Why didn't I think of that? I'll just pick one up on Kijiji.

 ≫ Ha ha. That's not what I meant. And it is easy. You already know a new guy—me.

 ○ Oh, right. You're probably some 60-year-old pedophile. As if I'm going to skip off into the sunset with Humbert squared.

 ≫ What's Humbert squared?

 ○ The weird pedophile in the novel *Lolita*. His name was Humbert Humbert.

 ≫ Oh, I get it. But I'm not a weird pedophile. Just a weird 15 year old. And not even really that weird. Brown hair, blue eyes. Grade 10 Student at Lawrence Park CI. B+ student. Play the French horn in the band. Play Starcraft whenever my little brother gets off the computer (he's a Club Penguin freak) and my mom forgets to yell, "Turn that blasted computer off!" And I play LPAA baseball every Monday evening at 6. First base.

 o Nice try. I almost believe you.

 ⊳Look, I know, I wouldn't believe me either. Actually, there's no way for me to know that YOU aren't the pedophile. Sucking in poor vulnerable kids like me to share their problems....

 o *laughing* So we have a Catch-22.

 ⊳What's that?

 o I guess you're not much of a reader, huh?

 ⊳Not unless I'm reading a web page. Total computer geek, I guess.

 o OK, me too. It's the title of an old book, but I only know it because it's mentioned in Green Day's song, "Walking Contradiction"—that's where I first heard about it. I had to ask my step-dad what it meant. He told me a Catch-22 is an impossible—and ridiculous—situation, sort of like being between a rock and a hard place. But dumber. So you call something a Catch-22 when you're caught in the middle, and there are no good choices or ways out. Like right now. We have no way of knowing if we are both for real or if one of us is a 60-year-old creep unless we meet. But we can't meet because one of us might be a 60-year-old creep.

 ▷I get it. But the problem is I really do want to meet you. Because if you are for real, and are really the person you sound like online, then I know we could really hit it off.

 ○ Whoa—RED ALERT!!!!! Not going to happen.

 ▷The 'city with the tall tower' you live in is Toronto, right? That's where I am.

 ○ LA LA LA—not listening...
Anyway, "Talk is cheap and lies are expensive./ My wallet's fat and so is my head." Same Green Day song.

 ▷You're a big Green Day fan? How about this, then: "Is it the cop, or am I the one that's really dangerous?"

∘ I know that—it's from "Warning." Cool tune.

 ⋙ Yeah. And what it says is that you can't be completely safe and actually live. You gotta break out of the bubble wrap sometime.

 ∘ Maybe so, C, but I'm not about to debubble myself with you, OK? We're doing just fine like this, with me on this side of the screen and you on the other. No matter where I live.

 ⋙ OK. You can play it like that if you want, but you never know what we might miss.
Listen. Here's my idea. Next week, let's say, Thursday, 5 PM. Do you have anything on then?

 ∘ Not that I can think of right now…Y?

 ⋙ I'm going to go to the Second Cup on Yonge, just north of Lawrence. It's not that far from my school, and it's on the subway line.
I'll sit at one of the stools in the window. I'll hold something in my hand so you can recognize me…
OK, what could it be? Thinking…thinking…
Got it. My brother left his copy of *Bart Simpson's Guide to Life* here by the PC. I'll take that. I'll hold it so that you can see it through the window.
You walk by the coffee place. Wear a green shirt or

something so I can recognize you. You can check me out, I can check you out. If we want to talk in person, you can come inside and I'll buy you a hot chocolate or something. Or you can keep walking. Your call entirely.

Whaddya say?

 ○ I say no freaking way am I agreeing to meet a total stranger in a public place. And you are making me totally nervous now, so I'm signing off.

 ≫OK, but I'm going to be there. I hope you decide to come. If not, I hope we can keep talking online at least.

 ○ I dunno, Crushed. I think I better stick to real live creeps. I'm starting to think you could be the virtual kind. Which is too bad because I liked having you as a virtual friend.

 ≫Live without warning, Bonnie! Take a chance? Please?

 ○ Bye.

Bonnie clicked the X and shut down her web browser. Her heart was pounding.

Was Crushed a pervert? She doubted it, but she had to recognize that there was a chance he could be. *It's what they do, isn't it*? Start chatting with you online, get you to trust them, then ask you to meet them.

But...

What if he was exactly who he said he was? A student at Lawrence? A regular kid from pretty well her own neighbourhood?

It kind of made sense that he would be. Bonnie and Jen had promoted the blog through Facebook, after all. It was only natural that the people who checked it out first would be their Facebook friends, or friends of Facebook friends. The odds, in fact, were in favour of the fact that Crushed was a perfectly normal fifteen-year-old North Toronto boy, just like he said he was. *And if he was...* Well, maybe something *could* happen. Something nice.

Not going to happen, Bonnie told herself. She stared ruefully at the desktop as the icons began winking off.

Jen came back into the room. "Any posts?" she asked distractedly as she climbed into bed.

Bonnie was glad Jen wasn't looking at her because that meant Jen wouldn't see her face when she lied to her.

"No," Bonnie said. "Blank, blank, and more blank."

"Doesn't matter," Jen replied, her voice soft and dreamy. "We've got enough on our own plates now...."

A moment later, she was asleep, her lips curling into a smile.

SURVIVAL SKILL #28:

DON'T FORGET TO BREATHE.

The next morning, Bonnie decided she had to come clean with Jen. She had to tell her that they had actually heard back from Crushed.

She bit the bullet and made her confession as they walked to school.

"...so that's it. I'm sorry I didn't tell you before. I just figured you had enough to think about without worrying about someone else's headaches. Especially since Crushed had more of a problem than homework and zits. Last thing you needed was to get worked up over our dumb blog."

"Oh, Bonnie, have you been stressing about this? It's OK. You were right—my head wasn't in it. But don't say it's dumb. It isn't dumb. The blog was a good idea. We wanted to help people, right? So when is that ever dumb? The only dumb part is that our own boring lives suddenly became a reality show. Survival 416: the Bonnie and Jen Burn Hour."

Bonnie was thoroughly relieved that Jen wasn't mad. She felt almost giddy. So she was smiling like the

Cheshire Cat when she said, "You know the funniest part? At one point, I actually thought Carter was Crushed. I was thinking he had the hots for me! Isn't that hysterical? Carter! And *me*!"

Jen suddenly stopped walking. "I don't see what's so funny about that."

"Oh c'mon!" Bonnie hooted with laughter. "Could you imagine having a thing with the Crinoid? That is just so gross! It was just so awful, and I couldn't even tell you!"

"There's nothing so terrible about Carter, Bonnie." Her voice was icy, like she had swallowed glass.

"What's got into you, Jen? This is Carter we're talking about. The Sleazetank. The Slimerator."

Jen turned on Bonnie. "OK, so maybe I said those things about him once. But that was before I knew him. I was going by what *you* had told me about him. But you know what? Carter is not like that. He's not a sleazetank, OK? He's a…"

She put her hands on her hips and her eyes blazed. She took a deep breath and exhaled through her mouth like she was gearing up for a fight.

"OK. I wasn't going to tell you yet," she said, "but I guess now's as good a time as any. You made your confession. Well, I've got one of my own.

"Last night, when you were typing to your virtual buddy, your real buddy, a.k.a. me, was really having a tough time. When I went downstairs, I was in pretty bad shape."

"Yeah, I remember. You went to get some warm milk."

"I poured some milk into a mug and put the mug in the microwave. While I waited for it to warm up, I felt like the whole world was crashing down on me. I couldn't take it—I started to cry. I sat down at the table and put my head down on my arms.

"Then I heard someone coming. I thought it was you. But it wasn't—it was Carter. Funny, he couldn't sleep either. I was surprised, but to tell you the truth, I was kind of glad it wasn't you. I knew you cared, but I also knew we'd somehow wind up talking about Paolo. And I was too miserable about my own life to be miserable about yours, too. "

Bonnie started to interrupt but Jen wouldn't let her. She just kept talking.

"He saw me sitting there and crying. He didn't say anything. He just came over and sat with me. He put his arms around me and stroked my hair, and he just let me cry on his shoulder. He was so nice, so sweet…and he was *there. He was there for me.* For the first time all week, I felt like maybe things were going to be OK. He made me feel safe. And I realized how he had been there for me *all week*. How everything he did was good and kind and thoughtful. I mean, yeah, he sometimes says stupid things—"

"Like *always*."

"He *sometimes* says stupid things," Jen said, her eyes narrowing, "but the truth is, he doesn't *do* stupid things. He does nice things.

"So I looked at him, and he looked at me, and we

realized that there was something more going on than just two friends sharing a good cry...."

Bonnie's stomach lurched.

"Go on," she said dully. There was a roaring sound in her ears. She felt faint.

"So, he kissed me, OK? And I kissed him! And it was really, really nice. And if I have any say in it, it's going to happen again. He told me he'd had a crush on me for some time. And I wasn't surprised because the truth is, I'd kind of noticed that underneath that 'frat boy' act he puts on, there was somebody really sweet...Yeah, I had noticed him, too. There. Now you know—so go ahead and call me a sleazetank, too."

"He had a crush on *you?*" Bonnie gasped. "But... but...that's impossible!" she stammered.

Jennifer crossed her arms over her chest. "Oh? It is? Is it really so impossible for you to believe that someone could actually be interested in me? Thanks a lot."

"I don't think that, Jen!" Bonnie said, stunned. "How can you say that? You're my best friend in the world!" Tears sprang to her eyes.

"Oh, am I? Or is it that I'm your *only* friend, Bonnie? You push everyone away from you—you don't let anyone in. Like Carter. You've pushed and pushed and pushed him away from the very first time you met him. You never gave him a chance. He could have been Brad Pitt and you would have run him down.

"And why? What has he ever done to you other than have the bad fortune to have his dad fall in love with your mom? It's not like it was such a picnic for him to have to leave his home and fit into yours. Did you try and make it easier for him? Nooooo—you barely gave him the time of day."

She shifted her backpack on her shoulders and started walking away from Bonnie.

"Jen!" Bonnie called after her, "Please wait!"

She could see Jen wasn't listening.

Bonnie ran after her. "Stop, Jen!"

She pulled on Jen's arm so she was facing her. "I can't believe you're saying this. You *know* I'm not evil like that! I'm just…shocked, I guess."

"Well yeah, you would be," Jen mumbled. "You can be so clueless, sometimes. You big goof."

She took a deep breath and ran her fingers through her hair.

"Look, Bonnie, Carter and I are probably going to be more than just friends now. I hope you can get used to it. That's all I have to say. You can do what you want from here on in—and I'm going to, too. And what I *want* to do now is get my butt to school before I get marked 'late.' Come if you want, or don't. It's your call." Then Jen shook Bonnie's hand off her arm and walked away.

Bonnie stood on the corner of Sheldrake and Mt. Pleasant, frozen. She couldn't move. She couldn't think. She didn't want to think. Going to school was certainly out of the question.

Feeling totally numb, she found herself turning on her heel and heading back up Mt. Pleasant toward home.

171

She retraced her steps to the house and let herself in. With exquisite care, she hung her backpack on its hook and slipped her jacket neatly on its hanger. She watched herself put one foot, and then the other, on the stairs, and let them carry her into her room.

Only when she was there, safe inside her cocoon, did Bonnie allow herself to cry.

Friday, aka *The End of the World*

So pretty well everything I thought I knew about the world is wrong.

GYNORMOUS ERROR #1. Carter is nice.

NICE ENOUGH so Jen can wind up KISSING Carter in the kitchen and LIKING IT.

GYNORMOUS ERROR #2. Jen, my best bestest bestest friend in the whole wide world, thinks I am selfish and clueless.

I feel like Alice in freaking Wonderland, trapped on the wrong side of the looking glass. From where I'm standing, everything looks just the same as it always does, except it's all inside out and backwards.

I can't stand it, any of it. I keep wishing I could transport myself magically to another mirror-world where my father is here, back home with us, Jen is at home with Tina and her dad, and Carter is dead. As long as I keep this magic vision in my head, I can stop myself from spinning down, down, into the black void.

But I just can't do it. The real world keeps hitting me WHACK between the eyes and forcing me back to the here and now, where I def do NOT want to be.

THIS SUCKS THIS SUCKS THIS SUCKS !!!!!!!

173

I've been going through every single conversation I've ever had with Carter in my mind. Could I really have been SO WRONG????

I've been lying in my bed, not answering the phone—stop freaking ringing already, I'm NOT answering you!!!—not doing much of anything but letting the events of my whole stupid life rewind before my eyes. It's a silent movie. I can see the lips moving, but I can't hear any words. I'm seeing the action unfold in front of me in jerky, faded colors, but the message is clear as day.

It's making me sick to my stomach because without the soundtrack (i.e., Carter's MOUTH) distracting me, I feel like I can actually SEE Carter. And he's not exactly the loud, obnoxious, dork I thought I knew.

The real Carter, it seems, tries to do the right thing but keeps blowing it because he doesn't know when to shut up. And sometimes, most of the time, he says annoying things. But Jen was right. Carter says stupid stuff. But he DOES the right thing.

PAINFUL EXAMPLE #1. The day Carter moved in. Giving me that awkward, goofy smile. Stopping to chat on the stairs. And me, breezing past him, ignoring him.

PAINFUL EXAMPLE #2. At the dinner table,

174

Carter passing the plates, helping to clear, tossing a donkey laugh over his shoulder. Me—arms crossed, refusing to give him the time of day.

PAINFUL EXAMPLE #3. Carter, eager to help when Jen and I were setting up the blog. Checking in regularly to see how things were going, begging with his eyes to be included. Me, giving him the brush off.

PAINFUL EXAMPLE #4. Carter, going out on a limb, inviting me to a party.

And Carter, at said party, taking care of me like I was a precious china doll. Shepherding me through the crowd of strangers, helping me get some food, making sure I was set up, comfortable. Wanting to talk.

In every scene with Carter, I can see myself too, and it isn't pretty.

What was it Crushed had written? Don't judge people by what they think, but by what they do.

And what had I written back? Talk is cheap.

So why had I been so busy judging Carter by the moronic things he sometimes _said_, instead of seeing what he _did_?

If I was honest with myself—and hey, this is surely a time for honesty, since I have nothing else left—Carter talks like a turkey, and acts like a man. Paolo on the other hand, talked like an angel and acted like a creep.

Add to that happy-joy-joy thought the lovely way Joe had described me: "shooting her mouth off like a Roman Candle every chance she gets."

Well, my dear brother Joe is right. How many dumb, stupid, thoughtless, mean, horrible things do I say in any given day? The truth is I'm not any better than Carter.

I've been so wrapped up in my own little drama, I never even noticed all the other dramas going on around me.

I have got to be the lowest, the worst, the most miserable human being on the planet.

SURVIVAL SKILL #29:

APOLOGIZE IF YOU ARE IN THE WRONG.

"Bonnie? Are you here?"
It was Jen.

She came pounding up the stairs and burst into the bedroom.

"Oh! Thank God," she said, placing her hand on her heart. She dialed in a number on her cell phone.

"Mrs. Molnar? Yeah, she's here. She's fine. OK. No—I'll tell her to call you. I'll talk to her first, OK? Thanks. No problem, really."

She snapped her phone shut and said to Bonnie, "When you didn't show up at school, no one knew where you were. The office called here, and when no one answered, they called your mom."

Tears sprang into Jen's eyes. She went over to Bonnie and hugged her.

"Oh, Bonnie! I'm so sorry! I should have never said those things to you. I was just so scared you were going to go crazy on me when I told you about me and Carter!"

Bonnie was crying, too. "No—you were right. I'm so

177

awful, I don't deserve you as a friend. I hate myself. I can't stand being me."

"Don't say that, Bonnie, please! I couldn't have survived this past week without you. You have to know that! What I said was just—"

"It was the truth, Jen. You're right. I am selfish and self-centred. And I think I have everything all figured out, but you know what? I know *nothing*. Zip. Nada. I'm sorry, I'm so, so sorry…" Bonnie sobbed.

"Shhhh," Jen said, rocking her in her arms. "Shhhh… Take a deep breath, come downstairs, and we'll make some KD. I don't know about you, but I could eat a flipping horse."

"Can we put ketchup on it?" Bonnie asked weakly.

"Go wild. Put sprinkles and jujubes on it if you want."

"I'm glad for you," Bonnie said. "And Carter. Really."

"I know," Jen said.

SURVIVAL SKILL #30:

THERE'S ALWAYS A SILVER LINING.

When Bonnie's mom came home from work, she promptly grounded Bonnie for the rest of the week. Jen asked her if Bonnie could be ungrounded by Saturday, since Carter had organized this whole Wonderland thing. Mrs. Molnar looked back and forth between the two girls a few times. Bonnie wondered if her mother had twigged to something going on between Jen and Carter, and if so, if she was thinking that she didn't want Bonnie to mess it up for them.

At last she said OK—as long as Bonnie was a "perfect angel between now and then."

Bonnie felt, in a way, that her mom's saying yes meant she was getting a second chance. That Wonderland was her opportunity to start over, fresh.

Beginning tomorrow, she resolved, she would think before she talked. Pay attention to the people around her. Be the new and improved Bonnie Bartels—older, and wiser, and kinder. *Definitely* kinder.

After dinner that evening, Bonnie went back up to her room to chill.

Her computer stared at her from the desk. *Was it only a week ago that they had so eagerly posted their blog?* What a jerk she'd been. To think she could actually help someone get through their problems, someone she'd never even met. How could she have been so arrogant to think she could save the 'starfish' of the world? She was nothing but a starfish herself…

Bonnie hit the power button. While she waited for all the programs to launch, she let her fingers rest lightly on the keyboard. They felt cold, lifeless.

At last, the hourglass disappeared and she was ready to roll. She clicked on the blog. There was a post from Invisible.

 Dear Bonnie and Jen,

Thank you. I called Kids Help phone like you suggested and they were really good. They hooked us up with an agency that sends out practical nurses to help moms and dads with disabled kids.

It turns out the nurse they sent has a kid that goes to my school. We've gotten to be pretty good friends and she's really been great. She knows how to make me laugh. When we're together, I feel like I can handle stuff a lot better.

My parents are doing better, too. They hadn't really realized how tough things had been for me since Bradley's accident, or that they had been neglecting me. They are just so worn out themselves, they didn't notice. It wasn't that they didn't care.

We made a new plan where one day one week, I go out and do something fun just with my mom. And the next week, I do something with my dad. It's only been one week so far, but it's still been really good coz this way everybody gets a bit of a break, right? Anyway, I know I don't know you for real, and we'll never probably get to know each other, but you were there for me when I needed a friend, so I guess that means you are true friends. I'll never forget that you two cared enough to answer my question. When I needed somebody to listen, you listened. And because you listened, I didn't do something really, really stupid that I would have regretted big time. Well, all I mean to say is I don't think I'll have to be writing to you again, now that I'm not so alone anymore. But I just wanted you to know. You helped me a lot.

Bye,

Your friend,

No Longer Invisible

A.k.a. Vanessa Tam

Friday (OK - the world's still surviving...)

I can't believe it! I'm so excited! We're all going to Wonderland!!!!!!

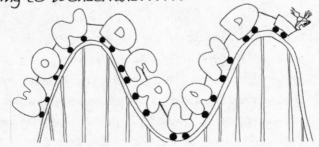

Carter—yes, CARTER—organized the whole thing. There's gonna be eight of us going: Jen and Carter (probably all lovey dovey ♡), Dan and me (maybe all lovey dovey? ACK! Gulp! ??? ♡ ♡ ???), and Joe with his date. Of COURSE Joe found a new girlfriend in about a nanosecond. He's like some kind of girl-magnet.

The girl is named Pascale and Joe told me she is one of Monster Mireille's friends. I kinda made a face when he told me that. I mean, any friend of Mireille's must be pretty monsteriffic too, right? But Joe said no. He said that Pascale had been at the mall the night M.M. had crapped all over him, but she wasn't one of the ones giggling or anything. And then, after one of his baseball games this week, she was there, waiting for him.

She told him she thought M.M. was just the biggest beeatch for doing what she did. And that she'd never do anything like that. You can guess the rest.

Pascale is bringing two of her friends, Rondi and Vijay. That makes a super fun-sounding group of eight. Which is good because if I have no freaking idea what to say to Dan, there will be lots of other people around so we don't wind up with one of those horrible awkward silences that st-r-e-t-c-h forever.

We're going to take the bus from Yorkdale and get to Wonderland about noon. That'll give us the whole afternoon and the whole evening at the park.

I'm so excited, I can hardly wait. I don't think I'm going to sleep much tonite.

b.o.n.n.i.e :) 1:36AM
What r u wearing 2moro

JEN.* <3 1:37AM
Clothes

b.o.n.n.i.e :) 1:38AM
Haha. Bringing swimsuit or wearing?

JEN.* <3 1:40AM
Wearing. Less 2 carry.

b.o.n.n.i.e :) 1:40AM
Which 1?

JEN.* <3 1:41AM
Pink 1. U?

b.o.n.n.i.e :) 1:42AM
The new 1. I'm so nervous.

JEN.* <3 1:43AM
Don't b. It will b fun.

b.o.n.n.i.e :) 1:43AM
Hope so.

JEN.* <3   1:44AM
UR Fab U will survive. And
FLOURISH! L8R BF

b.o.n.n.i.e :)   1:44AM
Luv ya

AMAZING DAY

I'm going to try and write this nice and slow. To try and relive _every single second_ as I describe it here. And then I'm going to read this over and over and over again _because_ _I can't believe what an awesome day it was_ _and how totally happy I am!!!!_

So we all decided we'd hang out at the water park part first, then do the rides later in the afternoon when it got cooler and the lines got shorter.

I was really nervous. Batshit nervous. You didn't have to be a genius to realize I'd be spending most of the day with Dan. Ga-gulp. No way could I forget what Carter had said: That _Dan kind of liked me._ I couldn't forget either that I had been a total tool at the dance and treated D like ca-ca. So my

186

hands were like ice and my mouth was so dry you could say <u>What is the Sahara?</u> and win valuable prizes. But what the heck, right? Nothing ventured, nothing gained!

So I laid out my towel on the grass next to Dan's and sat down. He didn't look at me, but now I knew it was because he was nervous as all get-out, and not because he thought I was hideous.

I looked around and realized Dan and I were the only people at the waterpark that weren't in our bathing suits. I knew I should take off my shirt and shorts—I was wearing my new stripey bikini underneath—but every time I thought about whipping off my shirt and sitting there practically naked, inches from Dan, it made me go all WAAAAHH!!!!

So I just pretended to look for something in my purse while Dan kept fiddling with his sunglasses cord and straightening and restraightening his towel even though it was already ruler perfect.

I thought having lots of people around would mean we wouldn't get stuck alone together, at least not right off the bat, but I was wrong. Everybody else had just thrown down their towels and taken off for the slide. So there we were Dan and me, side by side, two pathetic Nervous Nellies without a freaking clue about what to say to each other.

Can you say: AWKWARD????

I wanted to die. OK, not really. But I just wanted the awkward bits to be over already. I wished he would say something. Anything!!!!

Then Joe came running over and flicked some water on our faces.

He said, "The slide is awesome! Hurry up, we can all get in line together and go down one after another."

Right away Dan said sure. He got up and yanked off his shirt. I took a deep steadying yoga-style belly breath and yanked mine off too, then shimmied out of my shorts. We followed Joe to where you get the inflatable tubes, then got into the line for the super-slide.

The line was like a mile long. Joe and Vijay kept cracking jokes and that made me start to feel a little more relaxed. Rondi and Pascale were chattering away with Jen like old friends. Carter, meanwhile, had his arm around Jen's shoulder, and Jen looked so happy I half expected her to float up into the air any second.

I let myself actually look at Dan straight on for the first time. He had the cutest sprinkling of freckles across his nose.

They made him look just like a little kid.
SSSOOOOOOOO Cute!!!!

I can also add, since this is my
own diary and no one—this means
you Joe—is allowed to read it, that
D also has a Very Nice Body.

Dan looked up while I was still
looking at him and whhooops! It happened.
Our eyes met.

KABOOM!

And he smiled at me, and the way he smiled
was like

ZING A DINGA

Like sunshine breaking through the clouds
after a thunderstorm.

TWEET

TWEET

I can't believe I hadn't noticed at the
dance how absolutely adorable Dan is. He is
like a 9.9999 out of 10. What was wrong with
me that night? Did I not notice because I
wasn't looking? Or because he never smiled
at me like that?

Maybe both of us had been too nervous and too dumb to let our real selves show.

MISTAKE.
DO NOT REPEAT!!!

Anyways, I figured what was past was past, and none of that mattered anymore. What mattered is that we were there, right then, at Wonderland. Dan was smiling, I was smiling, and life was good.

It took FOREVER to make it up to the top of the slide tower, and only about twenty seconds to come down. But those twenty seconds were GREAT!!!!!!! We were all goofing around and splashing each other like insane porpoises, knocking each other down and whacking each other with the inflatables. And then we went right back into the slide line to do it all over again.

This time, Dan and I went down the slide 2gether. He sat behind me (!!!) and wrapped his arms (!) around my waist (!!!!) I was still nervous about being so close to him like that, but it was an OK kind of nervous. Don't ask me why, but I knew I could

190

trust him. The thing is, Dan isn't a Paolo.
<WHEW!!!!!> Maybe he doesn't have all the
right words to say and all the right moves.
And yeah, he can be shy, and more than a
little goofy. But underneath, he is a nice
person. And that's what counts.

Later, we headed over to the rides. Joe and
Carter wanted to go on the Minebuster.

Vijay announced that the last time he rode
it he tossed his cookies. So Rondi smacked
him and told him to ride in the next car back,
coz she wasn't going to ride with a barfer,
no matter how buff he was LOL!

I got in a car with Dan. My heart was
pounding like mad as the line inched its way
toward the entry.

Dan took my hand (!) in his (!) He asked me
if I was OK, and said we didn't have to go on
the coaster if I didn't want to, we could go
on the little antique cars.

I decided no, I wouldn't be a wusie, so I
took a breath and curled my fingers tighter
around his. I said, "No—let's go. You gotta
go for it sometimes, right?" And then he
said, "Yeah—live without warning, right?"

I couldn't believe my ears. What did you
say? I asked him and he repeated it: Live
without warning, you know, like in that old
Green Day song. He started humming it, but

191

really, all I could really hear was this loud
roaring in my ears. because that's exactly
what Crushed had said to me: Live without
Warning. Take a chance. Please?"

What a WEIRD coincidence—that Dan
would mention this exact same song and line.

I admit it—I was more than a little freaked
out. But then I just said to myself, oh get
over yourself. Dan isn't Crushed. He's just
an ordinary guy, quoting a really popular song.

And I realized, he could be my guy—if I
wanted him.

YES YES YES!

Dan must've seen the weird look on my
face, so he said, "What? Is something
wrong?"

"No. Not a thing," I said. I gave his hand a
little squeeze (!) and pressed a little closer
(!) to him (!).

"Yeah, let's go for it. Minebuster, here we
come!" I said. And off we went.

The rest of the day passed in a blur—
like one of those romantic montages they
show in movies. There we were, all of us
on the bumper cars, laughing and screaming
rude insults at each other. There we were:
Whirling on the Tea Cups. Goofing at our

grotesque reflections in the Fun House.
Tootling along the little curved path in the
antique cars. We went on every single ride so
many times that my head started to feel all
upside down and topsy-turvy.

And now we get to the Magic Moment...

We were on those
cute little Model T
cars.

Dan put his arm
around me.

I let myself wriggle
accidentally-on-purpose closer to him...

And then he took his other hand off the
steering wheel and OMG ran the back of his
fingers along my cheek.

"I'm glad I met you," he said. Then he
WRAPPED BOTH ARMS AROUND ME and
LET THE CAR DRIVE ITSELF for a while,
even though the wheels kept banging against
the metal guide rail ka-lunk, ka-lunk as the
car wandered on the track.

When we finally pulled into the "station,"
we were both red in the face and grinning like
morons.

The attendant winked and said "Nice driving,
bub," and "Keep your hands on the wheel,
next time, OK?"

193

It made me blush even worse.

Then we walked along the path, with Dan's arm around me and mine around him. I even slipped my hand into his back pocket (!), and leaned my head on his shoulder.

I told him what a great day it had been and he said, "The first of many I hope." Then, right there in the middle of the walkway, with families and running kids and the screams from the roller coasters swirling around us, he kissed me again. **WHOO-HOO!!**

I don't know if it was right then or a little while later, but it occurred to me that Carter was wrong. He once told me that he thought the way to survive was by detaching yourself from life. But I don't think that's it at all. The real way to deal with stuff is to become part of it, to jump in with both feet and not hang back, waiting for other people to make things happen for you. You gotta take a chance, take down the walls that keep you trapped in your own head and just let yourself go.

You have to smash through the mirror, break through the looking glass, and live.

○ Hi folks! If this is the first time you've clicked on this blog, you probably want to know how to survive something terrible.

 • We, your fearless bloggers, know an awful lot about survival. And to prove it, we'd like you to know that today is the official 100-DAY ANNIVERSARY of the launch of this blog.

 ○ During this past 100 days, we have learned even MORE about how to survive awful events that can strike an unprepared Middle Schooler/Junior High Student/Human.

 • Because we've been there.

 ○ When we started this blog, we already thought we knew about all the crappola that can happen to a person. We were wrong.

 • You can say now that we are definitely older and wiser.

 ○ Not that much older. But a TON wiser.

 • We think we were giving pretty good advice before. But now, we know our advice will be better than ever.

o Maybe, for example, from here on in it won't be quite so "black-and-white." This=good. That=bad. I've learned about all the shades of grey out there. Some are actually quite attractive.

 • And very flattering to your complexion, too, Bonnie, if I may say. That soft grey angora sweater makes your face look all glowy and rosy. But that could be the new boyfriend, eh?

 o Oh hush. *blushing*

 • In the past 100 days, I've learned that what doesn't kill you makes you stronger. And that no matter who you are, you never have to stop growing, or stop trying to improve. And no matter how old you are, not only will you survive, but you can do it brilliantly. I've also learned that we ALL need a helping hand sometimes. No one, anywhere, does it all alone. Which is actually a good thing, if you think about it.

 o Which is why we now want to say to all of you out there: If you have a problem, an issue, a question, a whatever: BRING IT.

 •Yup. Ask us anything.

∘ We will give you our very bestest advice on how to survive absolutely anything.

 • And if we don't have the answer, we will bring in some experts, like the awesome folks over at Kids Help Phone, who are now on standby to help us with the questions we are not qualified to answer.

 ∘ So you are 100% guaranteed, no, a billion percent guaranteed, to get the help you need so you can survive whatever you are going through.

 • That's a promise.

 ∘ And we all know, a promise is a promise, right? You will survive, we promise.

 ∘ • ABSOLUTELY ANYTHING! • ∘

Click <u>HERE</u> to ask Bonnie and Jen your questions on how to survive absolutely anything.

This Blog created and maintained by Bonnie B., who would never ever, EVER meet in person with someone that she met over the Internet. No matter how tempting. So you can relax, Mother Dear.

It's hard to believe Dan and I have been going out for almost three months!!! It's so crazy! When I think back to that day at Wonderland, when it all started, and then I think about now, I want to give my head a shake. It's like two totally different lives. And two totally different me's.

Jen is happy too. And not just because her mom seems to be doing really well in her new less-crazy job at the nursing home, but because of Carter too. And with Jen teaching Carter how to think first and talk second, well, he's turned out to be a pretty good catch, if I do say so myself. Who woulda thunk it?

Here's what happened. This morning, Dan texted me that he has something cool planned for our anniversary and it's going to be an awesome surprise. (!!!!!) He wants me to meet him at The Second Cup up north of Lawrence tomorrow at six pm sharp.

So there I am in math class, texting him back ok, when I suddenly remembered the last time I'd been at that Second Cup. It was back when Dan and I had only just hooked up. It was our third "date," I think, and there was a new pirate movie out that we both wanted to see.

He was hurrying me along, saying, "We can make the 6:30 show at Silver City but we have to hurry if we want to get something to eat first."

So he grabbed my hand and we raced down Yonge Street to the subway entrance. As we passed by The Second Cup, something made me hesitate. I slowed my step and glanced at my phone. It was 5:15. And it was Thursday.

"What?" Dan said.

"Hold on a second, there's something in my shoe," I fibbed, just to give myself a chance to think.

We walked slowly passed the plate glass window. I almost fainted. There was a boy sitting on the other side of the glass, on one of those stools that face the street. He had curly brown hair and he was wearing those neat John Lennon glasses with pink lenses.

I knew it had to be Crushed. The real Crushed. The guy from the blog.

He had wanted me to meet him there, at that very time and place. I squatted down and pretended to fish a pebble out from under my heel. I debated with myself what to do. Should I go in and talk to him? And if I did, what would I even say?

I glanced back up at the window. The boy

was gone!!! Where I thought he'd been sitting, there was just a young mom, her curly hair pushed behind her ears as she bent over a toddler, trying to get him to take his sippy cup. She was wearing sunglasses that reflected the light with a pinkish hue. Crushed, it turned out, had been nothing but a figment of my imagination.

I remember that Dan said, "Bonnie? You ok?" with this unbelievably cute, concerned look on his face. It made his forehead crinkle in that funny way I have come to love.

I stood up and gave him a big fat smile.

"Yeah, I'm fine. Sorry." I said. "That pebble was bugging me, but it's gone now. Let's go."

We walked hand-in-hand to the subway.

And you know what? I never looked back.